About the Authors

Frank Dirscherl (b. 1973) is the author and editor of the Amazon bestselling *The Wraith* and *Beyond the Lens*. His series of *The Wraith Adventures* books have been enjoyed by multitudes of readers the world over. Other books in the series include *Valley of Evil, Crossfire, Cult of the Damned* and *Cry of the Werewolf,* with more to come.

A professionally certified library technician, who has been working in libraries for twenty five years, Frank has also worked at a medical practice in a data entry position, covered books for a book wholesale company, as a lecturer to children on the merits, and writing, of comic books, and as an online activist for social equality.

He lives in the south coast of New South Wales, Australia, with his beautiful wife Jennifer, where he is currently working on his latest piece of fiction.

For more information on Frank Dirscherl, please visit his website at **www.frankdirscherl.com**

Bobby Nash may not spend his nights leaping from rooftop to rooftop while stopping crime like The Wraith, but he does spend his nights writing about characters who do. Bobby is an award-winning author of novels, comic books, short stories, novellas, graphic novels, and the occasional screenplay for a number of publishers and production companies. He is a member of the International Association of Media Tie-in Writers and International Thriller Writers. On occasion, Bobby appears in movies and TV shows. He always wins that Six Degrees of Kevin Bacon game.

Bobby was named Best Author in the 2013 Pulp Ark Awards. Rick Ruby, a character co-created by Bobby and author Sean Taylor also snagged a Pulp Ark Award for Best New Pulp Character of 2013. Bobby has also been nominated for the 2014 New Pulp Awards and Pulp Factory Awards for his work. Bobby's novel, *Alexandra Holzer's Ghost Gal: The Wild Hunt* won a Paranormal Literary Award in the 2015 Paranormal Awards. The Bobby Nash penned episode of *Starship Farragut*, 'Conspiracy of Innocence' won the Silver Award in the 2015 DC Film Festival.

For more information on Bobby Nash please visit him at
www.bobbynash.com

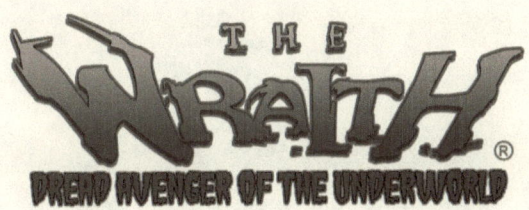

Praise for *The Wraith*
Amazon bestseller

"I love the coloring job and specially the 'glowing' eyes on the chest of the character."
- Guillermo del Toro, director, *Blade II, Hellboy I & II*

"I liked the story a lot... It's a very strong debut."
Steve Englehart, writer, *Detective Comics, The Avengers, Green Lantern*

"I have read the novel (I couldn't put it down)... It is amazing to see how her (Leena) character evolves from Part I to Part II. At first she appears as every other 'girlfriend' in an action film, but those twelve months that pass obviously change her as a person and I love the person she becomes: tougher, but still human."
- Amber Moelter, actress, *Catwoman: Copycat*

"I finished *The Wraith* book last night. I must say I enjoyed it quite a bit. The scenes kept playing in my head like a big budget Hollywood film. I mentioned earlier that I enjoy when the hero is put to the test physically and doesn't win the battle unscathed. Boy, (Frank) delivered that in spades!"
- Jeff Welborn, artist, *Nightmare World, The Wraith*

"Genius + sweat + dedication = hard hittin' hero action! Go Aussie!"
- Dan Lennard, writer, *People* magazine

"*The Wraith* is a wonderful throwback to the purple prose of the bloody pulps with a hero clearly descendant from the likes of the Shadow and the Spider. A fast, action-packed thrill-ride with great characters, both noble and villainous. Slam-bang kick off to a super new series. One I'm anxious to follow."

– Ron Fortier, writer, *The Spider, Brother Bones, Domino Lady*

"I became familiar with Frank Dirscherl's The Wraith from the comic book of the same name. When the first Wraith novel came out I just had to read it. I was not disappointed. The Wraith is a fast-paced thrill-ride. I'm looking forward to the upcoming sequel."

– Bobby Nash, writer, *Evil Ways, Fantastix, Lance Star*

"*The Wraith* (is) a really fun read. Have been a fan of Kenneth Robeson's Doc Savage and The Avenger books for years... *The Wraith* reminds me of Robeson at his best."

– G.R. Lawson, Publisher, General Jinjur Comics

"A short, pulp, superhero novel... Clearly more adventures to come with how this is set up."

– Richard Scott, *Super Reader* website

"*The Wraith* is an enlightening journey into the darkness of superhero fiction, and a worthy entry into both pulpdom and comicdom."

– Kevin Noel Olson, *Silver Bullet Comics* website

"*The Wraith* is a testament to Frank's dedication and talent. Other small press characters have come and gone, but The Wraith endures, because Frank understands what makes a classic character."

– Richard Evans, writer, *The Canadian Legion*

"When it comes to superhero fiction and classic pulp stories, Frank Dirscherl channels those classic adventures of the past into *The Wraith* with ease and gives you a hero to believe in."

– Stephen J. Semones, writer/director, *Beyond the Lens, Crossfire, The Wraith: Eyes of Judgment*

"Frank Dirscherl's writing is action-packed and reminds me why superhero fiction is so much fun in the first place!"

– A.P. Fuchs, writer, *The Axiom-man Saga, The Way of the Fog, Undead World trilogy*

"Totally enjoyed this book. Good story, a real hero vs villain yarn. Can't wait to read the other adventures of The Wraith."

– J. Newey, *Amazon*

Praise for *Valley of Evil*

"The second Wraith novel is an improvement, I think. Right from the start Dirscherl throws you into the middle of crazy action.... This book is a whole lot of superheroic pulp fun, and the good news is there seems to be more to come...I look forward to some more of the same."

    – Richard Scott, *Super Reader* website

"I think (Dirscherl) really captured a noir element with (his) voice."

    – Joshua Gamon, writer, *Abigail & Rox, Digital Webbing Presents*

"I did quite enjoy the books. Best of all, it wasn't overly sex-filled or gory—I can't stand most modern superhero comics that show such things or have the heroes just swear and swear. So *The Wraith* (and *Valley of Evil*) was just up my alley."

    – Greg Gick, writer, *The Werewolf of Rutherford Grange, Tales of the Shadowmen, Secret Agent X Vol. 2*

"The Dread Avenger is back. After battling the Cobra in his first prose adventure, The Wraith returns to face all new challenges from Metro City's greatest villains, most notably Hong Kong drug kingpin Ma Tzi. As with his first Wraith novel, Frank Dirscherl treats us to a pulp-inspired adventure that keeps readers on the edge of their seat. You have to read this novel in one sitting."

    – Bobby Nash, writer, *Evil Ways, Fantastix, Lance Star*

"In the past five years there has been a tremendous resurgence in pulp fiction centering on the old heroic pulps. Young writers have started taking up the mantle of old masters like Walter Gibson and Lester Dent and begun creating their own avengers in tales of genuine purple prose. Among the best of this new generation of wordsmiths is Australian, Frank Dirscherl and the exploits of his modern pulp paladin, The Wraith. This is grand pulp!"

– Ron Fortier, writer, *The Spider, Brother Bones, Domino Lady*

Praise for *Cult of the Damned*

"Only by the first three pages, Frank Dirscherl wonderfully captures a dark and mysterious atmosphere, one that leaves the reader with a cryptic and eerie sensation; one that makes me cold just thinking about it."

> – Rennie Cowan, writer/director, *The Thriller Idol: A Tribute to the Legacy of Michael Jackson, Kade the Conqueror*

"Frank Dirscherl pulls you into the world of The Wraith from the first sentence and refuses to let you go until the last one."

> – Stephen J. Semones, writer/director, *Beyond the Lens, Crossfire, The Wraith: Eyes of Judgment*

"The Wraith is one of my favorite characters and every time Frank Dirscherl puts pen to paper I know I'm in for a real treat."

> – A.P. Fuchs, writer, *The Axiom-man Saga, The Way of the Fog, Undead World trilogy*

Praise for *Cry of the Werewolf*

"Frank Dirscherl delivers beyond measure... The solid characters, settings and story really propel you page to page and leave you hanging on for more."

– Stephen J. Semones, writer/director, *Beyond the Lens, Crossfire, The Wraith: Eyes of Judgment*

"Each new installment in *The Wraith Adventures* series is a guaranteed good time filled with high adventure, romance and pulpy fun. Dirscherl is at the top of his form."

– A.P. Fuchs, writer, *The Axiom-man Saga, The Way of the Fog, Undead World trilogy*

Praise for *Zombies Attack!* in *Metahumans vs the Undead*

"This compilation of superheroes vs evil offers top entertainment for superhero lovers! Frank Dirscherl and others are at their best with their contributed stories. I will now pursue other stories written by these authors, such as those involving Mr. Dirscherl's The Wraith. This type of reading enjoyment knows no end!"

— Ramona Wingart, writer, *Where is Brother Beaver?,*
Emily Suzanne Smith!

Praise for *Werewolves Attack!* in *Metahumans vs Werewolves*

"Always a great read. Can never put it down once you get started... "

BY FRANK DIRSCHERL

FICTION

The Wraith Adventures series

Sanderson of Metro (with Bobby Nash)
Serpent Rising (with Greg Gick) – COMING SOON
The Wraith
Valley of Evil
Crossfire (edited)
Cult of the Damned
Cry of the Werewolf
Vendetta – COMING SOON

SHORT STORY COLLECTIONS

Metahumans vs. the Undead
Metahumans vs. Werewolves
Metahumans vs. Robots
Metahumans vs. the Ultimate Evil (with Adam Oravec)
Lance Star – Sky Ranger Vol. 1

NON-FICTION

The Wraith: Eyes of Judgment – The Official Script Book & Movie Guide
(with Stephen J. Semones)
The Hitchers of Oz
Beyond the Lens (edited)

COMIC BOOKS

The Wraith #0
The Wraith: The Collected Editions #1-3
Curse of the Cortes Stone (with Joe Martino & Scott Story)
Shadowflame: Bombed (with Joe Martino)

www.trinitycomics.com

BY BOBBY NASH

FICTION

Sanderson of Metro (with Frank Dirscherl)
Evil Ways
Alexandra Holzer's Ghost Gal: The Wild Hunt
Fight Card: Barefoot Bones
Earthstrike Agenda
Deadly Games!

SHORT STORY COLLECTIONS

Mama Tried
Domino Lady/Sherlock Holmes
The Black Bat Returns
Earth Station One: Tales of the Station
The Big Bad II
Gary Phillips' Hollis PI
The New Adventures of Major Lacy and Amusement, Inc.
Box Thirteen - Adventure Wanted
Zombies vs Robots: No Man's Land
The Spider: Extreme Prejudice
Lance Star – Sky Ranger Vol. 1-4
and many more...

COMIC BOOKS

Domino Lady Threesome #1
Edgar Rice Burroughs' At the Earth's Core
Big Bang Universe #1
Operation Silver Moon
Lance Star – Sky Ranger #1
All-Star Pulp Comics#1 & 3
and many more...

SANDERSON OF METRO

Books of Judgment Book One
a *Wraith Adventures* tale

by

Frank Dirscherl & Bobby Nash

TRINITY COMICS
WOLLONGONG

TRINITY COMICS
PO Box 31
Wollongong NSW 2520

ISBN 978-0-646-97923-6

PUBLISHED BY TRINITY COMICS, October 2017
www.trinitycomics.com
FRONT COVER PENCILS by Jeff Welborn
FRONT COVER INKS by Jeff Austin
FRONT COVER COLOURS by Splash!
COVER LAYOUT AND DESIGN AND INTERIOR DESIGN by Frank Dirscherl
EDITED by AP Fuchs

For more on *Sanderson of Metro*
visit www.trinitycomics.com

Text set in Garamond-Normal. Printed and bound in the USA

A catalogue record for this book is available from the National Library of Australia

The Wraith Adventures series in correct reading order (including short stories)

- *Sanderson of Metro* *
- *Serpent Rising* * - COMING SOON
- *The Wraith*
- *Valley of Evil*
- *Crossfire*
- *Cult of the Damned*
- *The Things I Love the Most* in *Metahumans vs the Ultimate Evil*
- *Cry of the Werewolf*
- *Werewolves Attack!* in *Metahumans vs Werewolves*
- *Sundown* in *The Wraith Dread Avenger of the Underworld* – COMING SOON
- *Swamp Witch of Satan's Forest Part 1* in *Sanderson of Metro* (hardcover edition)
- *Sanderson of Metro* *
- *Serpent Rising* * - COMING SOON
- *Vendetta* – COMING SOON
- *Robots Attack!* in *Metahumans vs Robots*
- *Zombies Attack!* in *Metahumans vs the Undead*

So far...

The story goes on...

* The novels *Sanderson of Metro* and *Serpent Rising* take place partially in the past and partially in the present, hence their multiple listings above.

To all you Wraith fans—this story is for *you* - FD

This one's dedicated to Stan Lee, Jack Kirby, Steve Ditko, and all the creators of super-hero fiction. Thanks for dreaming up all of these amazing four-color characters who inspired me onward and upward and taught me that great power and great responsibility go hand in hand. You have my eternal gratitude
- BN

SANDERSON OF METRO

~ Chapter 1 ~

It all started, as these things usually do, with a tip.

The Wraith was camped out atop a stack of shipping containers fresh off an incoming cargo ship from South America. From his perch he had an unobstructed view of the dock, the reason for his visit.

Docking slip twenty-three housed a freighter birthed out of Hong Kong. The containers had finished being unloaded twenty minutes earlier and were, according to the manifest that The Wraith had quietly taken a peek at, due for inspection at eight o'clock the next morning.

A small cadre of men and women had arrived just minutes after the last container had been stacked. A woman dressed all in black moved along the containers, scanning barcodes on the container hatches. Two men followed her, each heavily armed. The Wraith knew they were looking for a specific container out of the one hundred and forty that had just been unloaded.

The Wraith counted ten smugglers. Each was well armed, even the one driving the forklift.

"Looks like Jace was right," The Wraith whispered to himself as he watched the lady and her entourage continue to scan for their container.

The Metro City Police Department had been trying to get a workable lead on the smuggling operation for months, but all of their attempts had fallen short. Many believed the smugglers had someone on the inside, a police informant who warned them whenever MPD was getting too close. There was no proof, but it was the only plausible explanation that made sense. How else had the smugglers managed to stay three steps ahead of the police?

What they hadn't been able to stay ahead of was Jace.

Jace Rodriguez was a small-time crook The Wraith had busted a time or twenty over the past couple of years. As a crook, he was barely worth his or the police's time, but as a snitch, well, he was infinitely more valuable. Jace had the perfect super power for the job: as a lowly underling in the organization, he was all but invisible. People talked business in front of him all the time, barely even registering his presence. That's where his ineptitude as a career criminal worked in The Wraith's favor.

After busting him for the umpteenth time, The Wraith made Jace an offer too good to pass up. He would go to work for him and help him take down the criminals who preyed on the city or he was going to go away for a long time. Reluctantly, Jace agreed. He was smart enough to know it was his only real choice, that becoming an informant was better than a stint in prison, which is exactly where his next conviction would send him. With his record, Jace would have gone up the river for several years, a thought The Wraith knew terrified him.

Since then, Jace had come through for The Wraith on a number of occasions. His information was generally good and The Wraith had used it to finally help the Metro PD put a dent in the smuggling operation. There was still a lot of work to do, though, and The Wraith found himself once again at the docks on a hot tip.

The Dread Avenger stayed in the shadows, mentally clocking the positions of the smugglers below. Three were checking cargo barcodes, two stood guard next to the cars, another was across the way so he could keep an eye on the entrance. There was one man driving a forklift. The last of them was sitting behind the wheel, keeping the SUV they arrived in running. A box truck pulled in a few minutes later with a man and woman in the front. There might have been others in the back, but The Wraith could not tell.

On the face of it, the odds favored the smugglers, having sheer numbers on their side if nothing else, but The Wraith was no stranger to facing off against seemingly impossible odds and emerging victorious. He took no notice of such stakes.

The Wraith waited. Catching the smugglers was a win. The weapons they carried would be enough to arm a battalion. Heaven only knew the damage that could be done with such immense firepower. He had no intention of letting them, or anyone else, have such power. Not in his city.

However, he needed to catch them in the act. That meant waiting until they found the container they were looking for.

The woman slapped a hand against the container she had just scanned. She pointed toward the lock and one of the men with her rushed over with a pair of bolt cutters and, with minimal effort, snapped the lock.

The men pulled open the heavy metal door. It groaned loudly as the rusty metal hinges moved.

The container was full of pallets stacked two-high, each with cardboard boxes stacked six-high and shrink-wrapped to hold them in place. There was a corporate logo stamped on the boxes—TOSHI LTD. Some of the pallets also had a label on the outside of the shrink-wrap that read TOSHI UNLIMITED. These were the ones the smugglers seemed most interested in.

While the requisite pallets were being identified, the man driving the forklift unloaded eight pallets from the box truck. They were stacked two pallets high, all wrapped and labeled with the words TOSHI LTD.

It was an ingenious plan: Unload eight pallets from the container filled with illegal goods and replace them with eight identical pallets containing legitimate cargo that matched the manifest that would probably be taken as a holdover from the last shipment. That way, when the inspectors came by the next morning, there would be nothing out of place and the cargo container would pass without so much as a hint anything was out of the ordinary. The Wraith had to hand it to them—it was a smart plan.

And thanks to the tip he received, he caught it all on tape courtesy of the mini digital recorders he had placed around the area before the smugglers arrived. The Wraith would make sure these recordings found their way into the hands of Detective Bob Sloan down at Metro PD. Sloan would know what to do with them.

The Wraith looked forward to putting these smugglers out of business. They had been allowed to run unchecked for far too long. He was going to shut them down, and timing was everything.

Once the various pallets were unloaded and swapped over, The Wraith made his move. He quietly dropped to the ground, only his cape fluttering on the ocean breeze that cut through the narrow aisles between the containers like water through a hose. The narrow space was a tight fit, but not so much he couldn't move.

The Wraith stealthily came up behind the guard watching the entrance. He was the furthest from the group so taking him out wouldn't draw attention. He wanted to keep the element of surprise, and the guard was certainly surprised when a gloved hand clamped over his mouth and an arm tightened around his throat. The guard was jerked backward off his feet onto the gravel. A single punch took him down for the count. The Wraith pulled a thick, heavy-duty zip tie from one of the pouches behind his back and locked the guard's hands behind his back. He repeated the process for the man's feet before tearing off a strip of duct tape and slapping it across the man's mouth. Even if he came to before the cops arrived, he wouldn't be going anywhere and wouldn't be able to warn his crew.

Things had to move fast now.

The Wraith counted it off by the numbers as he had worked it out. Once the guard was down, he moved quickly toward the nearest SUV. The sport utility vehicles were made for smuggling. They had cargo room to spare and there was no shortage of them on the roads so they could blend in with Joe Q. Average on his way to work or the gym. The two SUVS were parked next to one another a short distance from the cargo containers so the box truck could park closer. There was only enough space between them to open the doors.

The Wraith dragged the bound guard into the narrow space, careful not to alert his two friends who were pacing back and forth next to the vehicles.

Although he still had the element of surprise working in his favor, taking down both guards before one of them could shout an alarm was tricky. The Wraith slipped three small gray pellets from a pouch on his belt and palmed them. Each pellet was roughly the size of a grape, but perfectly round. After much practice, The Wraith was stunningly accurate when he threw them.

Three pellets soared through the night sky, silent until they hit the gravel next to the guards and in front of the SUVs.

On impact, they activated, sending puffs of thick, dark gray smoke skyward.

The guards coughed.

The Dread Avenger of the Underworld moved swiftly and was on the run as soon as he had tossed the pellets. By the time the guards started hacking, he had already crossed the gulf between them and took the first down with a solid right cross that would make a Golden Gloves champion proud. A second shot put him down for the count.

Before his companion could compensate for the cloying smoke, The Wraith sailed over the hood of the first vehicle. He landed on the hood of the neighboring car and slid across it, his feet squarely landing on the wheezing guard's chest, knocking him to the ground. The gun clattered as it bounced across the gravel.

The Wraith grabbed a handful of the man's shirt and lifted him off the ground before delivering a knockout punch.

Quietly, he lowered the unconscious guard to the ground.

After zip tying both men and dragging them into the narrow space between the two vehicles, The Wraith turned his attention toward the box truck.

The driver was clearly an amateur, unlike the rest of the smugglers. He was casually seated on the driver's side, belting out tunes on the stereo in concert with the radio instead of watching his surroundings. He smoked an e-cig and had the window lowered to allow the noxious smell to seep out into the night air and mingle with the far stronger stench that permeated Metro's dockside area.

Definitely not a professional smuggler, The Wraith fancied, *but more likely a local hire.*

The Wraith figured that, if they needed a fall guy on the off chance things went wrong, it would be this guy offered up to the MPD. He noticed the punk was the only one not wearing gloves. Prints would be all over that truck.

Sometimes they make it too easy, he thought as he walked up beside the truck from the rear.

The driver was not even watching the mirror.

"Hi there," The Wraith said as he stepped up next to the window.

The driver let out a yelp of surprise, loosening his grip on the coffee that splattered all over him when it bounced off his knee.

The Wraith punched the driver through the open window, taking him out.

Moron.

The Wraith climbed on top of one of the cargo containers and made his way back toward the smugglers who were unloading it. The forklift driver had half of the pallets from the container. The woman in charge checked off each one as it was unloaded and set off to the side. The barcodes told her which ones to keep. With a tablet and a portable label printer, one of the men made replacement barcodes for the pallets that were to be reloaded onto the container in the swap. It was a smart operation.

The Wraith made his way between containers, which provided excellent cover. Once he reached the far end, he looked around the corner to get a bead on the smugglers' location. There were four of them. The woman in charge marked the crates she wanted to take with them. The two men with her helped the man driving the forklift to get them unloaded.

The Wraith climbed atop an adjacent container, out of sight of the smugglers, and waited. He watched as the last pallet was unloaded and they were about to start loading the ones they had brought with them into the container.

That was his cue.

The Wraith leapt from the container and landed atop the pallet of smuggled goods, the shrink-wrapped boxes cushioning his landing.

Understandably startled by the Dread Avenger's arrival, the forklift driver jerked the wheel hard and sent the vehicle sliding sideways on the loose gravel. The pallet hit a nearby container hard, but The Wraith was no longer there.

The Wraith leapt up, grabbed the top of the driver's roll cage, and swung feet first into the forklift cab, kicking the driver out and onto the gravel, the wind was knocked out of him.

The Wraith landed in a crouch on the driver's seat.

"Should've been wearing your seat belt," The Wraith said in deadpan fashion.

Before the winded driver could respond, gunfire filled the night air, bullets ricocheting off the forklift and container alike.

The Wraith dove out the rear of the forklift into a roll. He came up in a crouch and pulled three smoke pellets from his belt. With a simple flick of the wrist, the pellets flew through the air. Seconds later, a thick gas filled the area.

The forklift jerked to a halt as soon as pressure was taken off of the seat—a safety feature. It also supplied cover for The Wraith as the smugglers blindly opened fire into the smoke.

A wet *thump* followed by a scream told him that friendly fire had hit the forklift driver.

As the two men reloaded, The Wraith flew out of the smoke, and judging by the expression on his enemies, he looked every bit his namesake—a terrifying visage of avenging justice. He slammed into the closest gunman and knocked him to the ground before moving after the second man. Before he could react, The Wraith used the old one-two punch to take him out of the fight.

The first gunman groaned.

A pellet of sleeping gas landed on his chest, popped, and sent him to Slumberland.

"Hold it right there," the woman said. She pointed a large revolver at him.

"Look around you," The Wraith said. "Your team is down. It's all over."

"I'm the one holding the gun," she said.

"So...you're in control?"

"I'd say so." She motioned toward the open container.

Without her noticing, The Wraith quickly palmed a gas pellet.

"Inside," she told him.

"No," The Wraith said.

"Then you'll die."

"Won't be the first time," The Wraith said with a smirk as he flicked the pellet in her direction.

The gas pellet hit her center mass, popping on impact. A geyser of gray smoke billowed out, making her cough and spit.

The Wraith crossed the open distance between them in a shot, pulled the gun free from her grasp, and pushed her into a pallet of contraband inside the container. Boxes fell and busted open, revealing knockoff handbags and watches.

The Wraith took a menacing step toward her, the Eyes on his chest beginning to glow.

"Get away from me!" she screamed.

"You have information I need."

"You're getting nothing outta me!"

The Eyes of Judgment grew brighter until she had to shield her eyes due to their light.

"Your sins run deep," he told her. "I can help you. Justice must be served."

The woman screamed.

The Wraith's Judgment Stare roared to life, its light filling their immediate surroundings. Then, as suddenly as it flared, the light was gone and darkness fell across them.

The Wraith crouched in front of her.

She smiled.

"Now, before the police arrive, I have just a couple of questions," The Wraith said softly. "Will you help me?"

She nodded, never taking her eyes off the two eye symbols on The Wraith's uniform. The Eyes of Judgment had changed her—had saved her.

"Of course," she said. "Anything you want."

* * * * * *

From a perch high atop one of the cranes, The Wraith watched while MPD detectives Bob Sloan and Rosa Perez oversaw the arrest of the ten smugglers. They were loaded into a paddy wagon to be shipped off to the station for processing.

Catching them with the smuggled objects plus the files The Wraith had surreptitiously forwarded to their attention, along with the footage of them caught in the act—which was now being loaded onto the dock's closed circuit television backups—the police would have no reason to believe the security's CCTV video had come from anywhere except legitimate means.

Once he was convinced the MPD had everything in hand, The Wraith slipped away and headed for home.

* * * * * *

Home for The Wraith usually meant the Lair. That night, however, his journey stopped short of the hidden entrance to his secret base of operations within the center of Sanderson House, the great mansion located on a large estate within the heart of the city.

The Wraith walked across the freshly-manicured lawn toward a section of the Sanderson estate that was not often visited by anyone other than him and the landscapers. Thunder roiled in the distance, threatening morning showers for those poor souls on their early commute to work.

"Hi," he said once he reached his destination.

There was no answer, of course. He hadn't heard his— *Paul's*—father's voice since...was it Africa? That seemed so long ago, especially since it wasn't a life he lived, but remembered as vividly as if he had.

The headstones for Robert and Anna Sanderson were immaculate, chiseled from the finest hunks of marble money could buy. The stones that marked their graves matched the life the parents of Paul Sanderson had lived—one of excess and status.

Next to the ornate headstones, a third grave was vaguely visible, though no headstone marked the passage of the brave man buried there. It would be impossible to explain how Paul Sanderson could be buried next to his parents while he was also very much alive and living in the main house.

The Wraith looked down at the watch in his hand; he must've taken one and not realized it. The fake Rolex Submariner wasn't anything special. He wasn't even sure why he had taken it from the crime scene. That was a lie, of course. He knew *exactly* why he had absentmindedly taken it.

"It reminded me of you," The Wraith told the headstone of Robert Sanderson, his predecessor's father, a man he had never actually met but nevertheless felt and remembered as his own. "I've been thinking about you a lot of late. I wonder what you would think of the man your son became. Would you be proud of him? And of me, his successor, acting in his name?"

Only silence answered him, as it always did when he visited.

He looked down at the unmarked grave and felt a pang of sadness.

"I haven't forgotten, Paul," he said. "The mission continues."

The Wraith turned his back on the graves and walked as the rain began to tumble down.

~ Chapter 2 ~

Leena Patterson stood in front of one of the large bookcases in Paul Sanderson's study, her shoulder-length strawberry-blonde hair freely cascading down.

The big mahogany bookcase that ran the length of the room had always impressed her. Not only because of the rare first editions she found there or the selection of classic literature that rivaled more than a few prestigious libraries, but that they were shelved side by side with modern thrillers, pulps both old and new, and graphic novels. The dichotomy of Paul's shelving system was as unique as the man himself. Paul Sanderson was a contradiction at times, a mystery at others, but those small little quirks were part of what made her fall in love with him before the cape in his former guise of Michael Reeve, and again after he adopted his new identity.

The modern era novels, mostly crime thrillers, were the only items in the room that did not look as though they were holdovers from the past, trapped forever in a moment. Everything else looked like the type of place where a famous detective like Sherlock Holmes might feel at home. Sir Arthur Conan Doyle's classic detective was a favorite of Paul's and there were multiple copies of each on the shelf. There was even a Stradivarius on a display stand in the study she assumed belonged to the original Paul Sanderson's father since she'd never heard him play a single note on it.

Leena selected a specific book from a section of the shelf. It was the only book in the entire room she had never been able to read. According to the name etched on the spine, *Murder Chimes at Midnight* was written by S.N. Aderson, an author she had never heard of, one she assumed was made up. S.N. Aderson was no doubt a clever anagram of the Sanderson family name.

She gave the novel a soft tug.

A hidden mechanism behind the shelf unlatched and it silently slid open, revealing the hidden entrance to the lair of the Dread Avenger of the Underworld, The Wraith.

She smiled as she stepped through the secret door. This method of opening the Lair entrance was rarely used since Max Horton, The Wraith's right-hand man, a gifted engineer and mechanic who also acted as the Sanderson chauffeur and whom the original Paul Sanderson had met and befriended some years back, invented a handheld remote control to achieve the same function. Leena enjoyed using the old-fashioned latch from time to time, however. Watching the bookcase slide open still gave her a thrill.

She preferred to take her morning coffee in the study with Paul, if he was working, or in the kitchen, but this morning she flew solo. Whatever mission had kept him occupied the night before must have been a taxing one since he hadn't come to bed. She wasn't even certain he had come home, which on occasion didn't happen. He would call when he could, but sometimes there just wasn't time, especially when he was in the thick of danger.

It was still too early to worry, or worry any more than she usually did when The Wraith was on the prowl. She hoped he was down in the Lair, caught up in whatever mystery his masked identity had conjured up and simply oblivious to the time. That, too, was not unusual.

There was never a shortage of trouble for Paul, or his alter ego, to find in Metro City.

The Victorian feel of the study appealed to her. It was warm and welcoming, the exact opposite of the Lair, the room where Paul seemed to spend most of his waking hours when he was deeply concerned with whatever ailed the city.

The Lair itself was cold and sterile, almost utilitarian in its starkness. Little thought had been placed on aesthetics when it came to designing the place. This was where the cold hand of justice waged its never-ending war on crime, and the design echoed that cold hard feel.

The Lair was filled with state of the art components that would have been the envy of any forensics lab in the country. Computers, scanners, gadgets, drones, and heaven only knew what else was stored throughout the Lair. All of it had either been purchased with money from the Sanderson family trust or created virtually from scratch by Max. On Leena's first visit to the Lair, it was already stocked and ready to go. Her Paul had made a few minor adjustments since, but it remained as functional and stark as ever.

As she had guessed, Paul was there, still in his Wraith uniform, pacing back and forth as was his wont when troubled. She waited patiently, watching carefully. Her heart cried out for him, but she knew better than to break in on his thoughts until he was ready.

Leena hadn't even noticed her mind had wandered onto the details of the day. It wasn't until the *THUNK!* of the watch landing on top of her desk snapped her back to the here and now that she even realized she'd taken her attention away from The Wraith. He turned to face her.

She started, but quickly recovered. "Is everything all right?" she asked, staring up at him.

"You're right, Leena," he said.

"I am?"

"Of course," he said around a hint of a smile. "You usually are, you know."

"You'll get no argument from me," she said as she tried to play off the fact she hadn't been listening. She pushed her glasses up on her nose, a nervous tick. "And, uh...what is it I'm right about this time?"

"I think it's time I told you everything."

* * * * * *

The Wraith let out a breath he didn't realize he'd been holding.

"This is a story I've never told anyone, Leena," he said, leaning on the railing and staring up at the Lair's upper level toward the exit to the study. "Not even Max or Simpson knows the entire truth. Not really. They know part of it, but not the whole story."

Leena appeared as though she wanted to say something, to perhaps comfort him, but chose otherwise. She glanced at the watch lying on the workbench.

He took a deep, cleansing breath, then let it out. "You know all about my life as Michael Reeve," he said, referring to the man he had been before assuming the mantle of Paul Sanderson and The Wraith upon the original's death.

She nodded.

"But I've shared very little about Paul Sanderson's life before he and I crossed paths. As smooth as the memory transfer was that put me here, it's still a little strange recounting a life that wasn't really mine." He stared off into nothingness a moment. "Yet it was my life...after a fashion. It feels like my life, my memories."

Leena reached down and touched the watch, picked it up, and examined it.

"Sometimes I feel as fake as that watch," he said when he saw it in her hands.

"Chinese?" she said as she examined the watch's lines.

"Taiwanese, I'd wager. From there it was smuggled out of Hong Kong to Metro City on a cargo ship."

Leena humphed. "That's a well-traveled knockoff."

"Indeed it is. And it was probably the least dangerous item in the shipment. Metro PD took possession of the guns, the drugs, and all of the various knockoffs like the watches early this morning."

"And you decided you needed a souvenir?"

He turned to face her, uncertain he had heard her correctly.

She held up the fake Rolex and gave it a little shake.

"Hardly," The Wraith said. "I didn't even realize I had taken it until I got back home and sat it down on the desk and saw you standing here. I almost brought you a fake Gucci handbag, although they spelled it Guccie with an E."

"Is the watch a clue to some bigger mystery?" Leena asked. "Maybe a link to the person behind the smuggling ring?"

"No. Nothing of the sort."

"Then why did you take this watch?"

His mouth tightened. He walked over to the wall and touched one of the panels there. With a soft *click*, three sides of the panel popped open like a door. It was just one of many nooks and crannies that had been designed into the Lair where he could hide whatever he needed and keep it squirreled away for a later date. He had hidden her birthday gift in one such cubbyhole last year so she wouldn't "accidentally" stumble across it.

The Wraith pulled a small box out of its secret resting place. He held it gently, almost reverently, as he carried it over to her desk.

Carefully, he handed her the box.

It was small and opened on a well-oiled hinge in Leena's hand. Inside was a small piece of cheesecloth wrapped around something metallic. Seemingly seeing how he had handled it, she delicately moved aside the covering to see what it was that deserved to be hidden away so carefully.

It was a Rolex Submariner watch, the no date pre-ceramic bezel version, in pristine condition.

"It's beautiful," she said.

"It belonged to Paul Sanderson's father, a late pre-ceramic version. He inherited the watch when his father died and I...when the first Paul Sanderson died...it became mine. It's been in that drawer since he returned to Metro City. He—and I—haven't been able to even look at it, let alone wear it, ever since."

"I'm sorry. I didn't know."

"How could you?" The Wraith said.

"It's obviously very important to you."

"It is. It's the best memory I have of my—of Paul's—father. I never actually met the man, but I feel his presence every time I look at that watch. That's why I keep it locked away, out of sight. But tonight on that dock..."

His mind drifted, racing back through the night's events. Everything was a blur then, but now it all played back in slow motion. The smugglers, the dock, the contraband, the–

The watch.

"When I saw that watch, it all just came tumbling back on me. It was all I could do to not be overwhelmed by it. Father's watch.... I knew it was a knockoff as soon as I saw it, of course, but it's close enough to the real thing."

"It's in perfect condition," Leena said. "Not cheap."

"He could afford it," The Wraith said with a hoarse croak.

"Want to talk about it?"

He took the watch from her and looked at it. He had never felt right about wearing it. He had, for a time, considered it, but could never bring himself to do so.

"It might make you feel better," she said.

He blew out a breath. She was right, of course, as he had told her. It was one of the things he loved about her. She knew him better than anyone and still cared. It was a rare gift, one he was not so certain he deserved.

He blew out another breath.

"Like that watch, the story of Paul Sanderson is a strange one, but I think it's a story worth telling if you would like to hear it," he said.

Leena laid a hand on his arm, clearly letting him know she was there for him, ready to listen.

He flinched slightly. Even after all the years, the pain of what had occurred was still strong.

"You know you can tell me anything," she said softly.

The Wraith smiled. "I know, Leena. I'm sorry, but I guess I've put it off so long I was afraid to say the words out loud. But now that I am truly Paul Sanderson, I want you to know everything about me, all of me."

Leena sat down at the workbench and got comfortable. Paul knew they'd be there for some time.

"Where to begin..." he said.

"The beginning is usually a good place to start."

"You're right," he said with a small chuckle. "Again." He shifted to and fro, thinking briefly before starting. "Okay. Well, as you know, the Sanderson family made its money in real estate and the stock market."

"Yes."

"At one stage, long before Robert Latham came along, they owned most of this city, including the downtown corridor. Robert and Anna Sanderson were pillars of Metro City society, fixtures at thousand-dollar-a-plate fundraisers and charity galas. Paul never knew what cause was so near and dear to their hearts as they seemed to change on a whim."

"I" —he cleared his throat to cover his gaffe— "Paul Sanderson was born into a life of wealth and privilege. Everything he wanted he got. Everything save what he really craved, the one thing that would have made him happy— loving parents. Did you know that when he was ten, his best friend was an imaginary one? It's true. They played with action figures and building block sets while his parents were off saving the world's children, completely ignoring their own child."

The Wraith stared blankly above for a moment at the memory.

"Young Paul tried everything to get their attention," he said. "He studied hard, brought home good grades, even going for extra credit as if that would help put him in their good graces. When he was ten, he made the baseball team at school. Surely, his father would be impressed by that accomplishment. It wasn't to be. 'But you promised you'd come see me play today,' Paul told him, trying hard not to cry in front of his father. 'Sanderson men don't show emotions,' he remembered his father telling him once after his bicycle had crashed and he had skinned his knee."

The Wraith paced back and forth.

"'I'm sorry, son,' he had said to Paul, 'but you know how busy I am with work. And your mother...'"

The Wraith let out a soft, sad chuckle.

"All Mother could say was, 'Simpson will be happy to take you again, dear.' And so he did. He and Simpson enjoyed many a game together, and as much as Paul appreciated his being there as he got older, that little boy only saw him as someone who was not his father. Eventually, Paul came to realize Simpson was probably the closest thing he had to a real dad."

Leena sighed. "I had no idea."

"Try as he might, nothing Paul did could ever rouse his parents from their own lives except when they were rushing him to get ready or get moving when they needed to show off their precious son. Paul tried to enjoy those moments, false though they were. It was the closest he would get to having the family he wanted."

"That's terrible," Leena said.

He smiled. "He got used to it."

"But he shouldn't have had to. No one should."

"You'll get no argument from me, but poor Paul...Paul grew up feeling aloof and different. Alone."

Sanderson men don't show emotions. Paul's father's words rung out in his mind.

The Wraith turned to face her. "It wasn't all bad. Unlike most kids, there was no one telling him to go to bed on time or to eat his vegetables, although Simpson certainly tried." He smiled at the memory. "Paul spent a good deal of time reading. With Simpson's help, young Paul built a small tree fort in that big oak out back. They camouflaged it well. Paul's parents were never wise to its existence. Somehow, I don't think they would have approved. He must have read every book in the family library, not to mention every book at the school and public libraries as well. Reading was an escape. In the pages of a book, he could go on adventures unlike anything he had ever before dreamed. They were his way out, how Paul escaped his life. He was especially fond of reading about heroes. Real life or fantasy, they truly captured his imagination."

Paul pulled off the cowl and ran his hands through his tussled hair. "I think it was reading about those heroes that made Paul decide upon The Wraith persona." He noted the confusion in Leena's expression. "But I'm getting ahead of myself," he said with a smile. "There were a lot of years between that tree fort and becoming the Dread Avenger of the Underworld."

He took a seat beside her before continuing. "School might have been an opportunity for a more normal life, where young Paul could mix with children of his own age and make friends, but he was as much an outcast there as he was at home. The kids were so.... I guess 'jealous' is the word. They rode buses to school while Paul was driven there in a stretch limousine by his own personal driver. Simpson called him Master Paul out of deference. The kids at school called him the same thing because they thought it was hilarious. Or maybe they just liked to see him cry."

The Wraith rubbed his chin, remembering one of the many fights young Paul found himself in as a child. "Unlike when I wear this costume, back then he didn't know how to fight; only how to run away from the bullies."

"Kids can be cruel," Leena said.

"So I've heard," Paul said behind a pained smile. "Understand, I...he...was still a young boy. There had been no one to teach him how to stand up for himself. He had never been given fatherly advice on how to deal with a bully. He wanted to be like his schoolmates, but no matter how hard he tried, he could not make friends. It wasn't until he reached his teens that he truly understood deep down he was different than those he went to school with."

"Different? How so?" Leena asked.

"Just...different. The normal life of other children—of other people—he decided this type of life was perhaps not for him. Of course, if not, then what life was there for him?"

"What did he decide?" Leena asked.

"Nothing."

"Excuse me?"

"Paul didn't have any answers then, and even if he did, he would have been afraid to reinvent himself. If he wasn't the son of Robert and Anna Sanderson, the king and queen of the Metro City social scene, then who was he? For a while, he learned to put up with not knowing, but eventually, answer or no, he knew he had to go in search of something. In search of himself."

"Poor thing."

"At first, he thought college might have some answers, but..." He stood, once again leaning up on the nearby railing that separated the main section of the Lair from Max's engineering lab. He gazed at Leena and knew he had to go on with his story.

~ Chapter 3 ~

"The upside to having money was being able to attend the college of your choice," Paul started again. "After realizing that going to college was just like going to school—and that it was expected of him by his parents—Paul gave up caring which college he went to. At that point, he was less interested in experiencing college life or getting a quality education than he was in just getting through it and getting out into the world. That attitude did not sit well with his father, who tried to persuade him to reconsider his choice for higher education. His arguments fell on deaf ears."

Paul turned to face Leena. "Paul had made up his mind and he was determined not to change it. If there was one thing Robert and Paul Sanderson had in common, it was they both shared a stubborn streak as long as the Metro Bridge. Once either of them had set their minds to something there was no changing it, no matter how compelling the argument. They would both just as soon stick to their guns even if they knew they were in the wrong just to prove a point."

"I've seen this first-hand," Leena said with a smirk.

Paul acknowledged her with a smirk of his own. "Metro University sat on the outskirts of Metro City, as it still does. A sprawling campus that covers eight hundred and twelve acres of prime real estate an hour and a half's drive north of downtown. His decision to remain in Metro City instead of a more prestigious institution only widened the divide between him and his father, who had expected him to attend Yale like his father and grandfather before him." Paul sighed. "The last word's Robert Sanderson said to his son before he departed for college was 'You need to wake up, son!' They went a year without speaking before his mother finally reached out to him."

Leena shook her head in what appeared to be sorrow.

"On the one hand, Paul had been happy to hear from her. She was his mother and he loved her. On the other, he sometimes wished he had never answered the phone when she called."

"So," Leena said, "college didn't provide Paul with any answers? Any point to his life?"

Paul shook his head. "He was one of the forty-one thousand new students at Metro University when he walked onto campus that year as a freshman. He thought it would be easy to get lost in the shuffle there, that he could be just another face in the crowd. Get in there and get it over with." He paused in silent thought.

Leena perked up. "And?"

"He was wrong. All wrong. Fraternities and college boosters were like bloodhounds when it came to sniffing out wealthy freshmen. They pounced on Paul the moment he stepped foot on campus. He had his pick of fraternity houses or activities. All that was needed was a 'small donation,' and they all had their hands out. Everyone seemed surprised when Paul turned each of them down and got himself a small apartment off campus where he lived alone, away from their haggling. Eventually, most of them stopped trying to pledge him, but not all. Some were too stubborn to know when to quit. These he tried to give as wide a berth as possible."

Paul started pacing again. "By the end of his first semester, Paul started to relax a bit...but only a bit. The time away from Sanderson House and the trappings of wealth and social standing had begun to fade, and his teachers and classmates had started to treat him, if not like just another one of the guys, they at least left him alone. He was doing well in his classes; he was highly intelligent after all, but he wasn't putting that much of an effort in. When all was said and done, college life wasn't for him either. As I said, he found no answers there for the gaping hole inside of him."

Paul stopped and faced Leena. "The search continued."

* * * * * *

METRO CITY UNIVERSITY – TEN YEARS EARLIER

"Hey, Sanderson!"

It was a sunny, perfect day when one of Paul's classmates called out to him as he walked across the quad on his way to class.

Paul turned to see a student running his way across the crowded campus lawn. He did not know him well, but recognized the boy from his Political History class. He was a football player and wore his Letterman's jacket even though the temperature did not require it. Most students had opted for shorts and short sleeves.

"Glad I caught you," the jock said as he puffed to catch his breath.

"Do you need to sit down?" Paul asked. He could not recall the guy's name.

The jock laughed, clearly mistaking the honest question for a joke. "Nah, man. I'm good. Guess I need to lay off the cigarettes between classes."

"Probably a good idea."

"Right," the jock said. He wore his best car salesman smile.

"You wanted something? I'm kinda late for class."

"Oh, right," he said, chuckling. "My fraternity is looking to pledge some new members and I thought you would be a great fit. You've got the grades and can afford the rent and dues. What do you say? Ever thought about joining Alpha Pi Delta?"

"Not really," Paul said bluntly. He had watched how the fraternity guys acted since he got there. The ones he had witnessed were boorish at best—especially toward women—and were nothing more than bullies to those who were not associated with college sports teams, and even a few who were. He knew it was his family's wealth that had kept that particular bullseye off his back. The jock's fraternity was made up mostly of trust fund babies and athletes on full scholarships who were getting kickbacks and gifts from pro teams that were scouting them. Plain and simple, Paul knew Alpha Pi Delta didn't want him as much as they wanted his family's money and influence and he had little desire to give them either.

"Sounds like...fun. I appreciate the offer," he lied. "Unfortunately, I'm going to have to pass on the opportunity. I hope you understand."

"I don't," the jock said, his smile turning to a scowl.

"Sorry."

Paul started to walk away, but the jock grabbed Paul by the arm and jerked him back around so they were face to face. Paul dropped his books.

"Who the hell do you think you are, huh?" the jock shouted. "You think you're too good for us, is that it? Look around, man. There are two kinds of people in this world. There are the sheep," he said, motioning toward the clusters of students on the lawn—some reading, others tossing a Frisbee back and forth—then thumped his chest with his big ham fist. "And there are leaders!"

Paul stared at him.

"You could have that power, Sanderson. All you have to do is reach out and take it like your father did. Is he a sheep or a leader? From what I've read about him, he's a man who knows how to get things done."

"I'll have to take your word on that," Paul said candidly.

"What are you afraid of, Sanderson?"

"I don't have time for this," Paul said and pulled—and turned—away. "You can take your precious fraternity and your power and shove it up your ass!"

"How dare you?" the jock started.

Paul spun back around to face him, a finger held up to silence him. "You stay the hell away from me! Got it?"

Paul walked away. He turned briefly, noticing the jock whose name he still couldn't recall staring open-mouthed at him. Paul had no interest in joining them or *anyone*. He thought he had made that perfectly clear, but apparently some of his fellow students were slow learners. He knew that turning down the Alpha Pi Delta frat brothers meant the bullseye he had so far avoided would start searching for him. He wasn't worried though. He might not have an interest in social niceties or getting to know his fellow classmates, but Paul Sanderson had been training with private tutors since he was ten. Simpson had suggested martial arts and exercise as a way to work out his frustrations over his parents' lack of attention.

As always, Simpson was right. Training helped him keep focus, and Paul had become quite adept in his skills. If the frat brothers came after him, they would be in for a surprise.

As it turned out, it didn't take long for them to make their move.

A gang of brutes jumped him two nights later as he walked back to his off-campus apartment.

There were five of them, all dressed in black with ski masks and hoodies.

Not the most original look, Paul thought as he broke one of the attacker's arms.

The fight was quickly over and Paul continued on to his apartment with only bruised knuckles to indicate he had done anything other than take a stroll across campus.

In his first period class the next day, some of the Alpha Pi Delta boys came in bandaged, limping, and otherwise battered. Three had black eyes and one of them sported a new plaster cast on his left arm. The five of them spun a sordid tale about running across a gang coming back from the local strip club the night before. Paul merely smiled upon hearing that.

* * * * * *

"College passed by like a blur of classes from then on," Paul said, "all studying, parties, drinking, fighting, and sex. Despite Paul's constant dour demeanor, he still managed to get to know people—none he would think of as close friends—but acquaintances nonetheless. He faked his way through social situations, watched the room. It was studying his fellow man closely that taught him the invaluable art of reading people. If you watched intimately enough, their tells became apparent and they unwittingly gave away their secrets."

Paul paced again. "Paul was a rich, good looking, young man so there was no shortage of women eager to spend time with him. He had hoped the companionship would help fill the emptiness inside him. It didn't. Even the sex became a chore after a time. He yearned to know what made him different. Even taking into account his lonely upbringing, he knew there was something more to life than the one he was living, and college wasn't supplying the answers he needed. He knew there had to be something for him out there, somewhere in the world. All he had to do was find it. As soon as the moment presented itself, Paul Sanderson left college behind him and set off on a journey that would change not only his life forever, but it would also change the life of a man he had not yet met. A man named Michael Reeve."

~ Chapter 4 ~

"**H**itting the road was the best decision Paul Sanderson ever made," Paul said, continuing to shuffle back and forth before Leena, who intently listened to every word.

"Paul traveled, searching for whatever it was that would complete him and give his life some meaning...some purpose. Although he did not know what it was he was missing in his life, he believed the answers he sought were out there...somewhere. All he had to do was find them. His travels started in Paris. It wasn't for any one particular reason. Paris was one of those magical cities he had read about but never experienced, and when he arrived at the airport, the next flight out with open seats was to Paris. He would begin there and see where the fates would take him."

"Mmm, Paris," Leena murmured. "I'd love to go there myself."

Paul smiled but said nothing in reply, preferring to continue with his tale. "After spending two days exploring Paris like a typical tourist, Paul loaded up his backpack with supplies purchased in the city and a sleeping roll, and hit the road. He walked a great deal of the time, in no hurry to get anywhere. At other times he hitchhiked, rented bicycles, motorbikes, horses, and at least in one instance, rode on an ornery camel he nicknamed Popeye after his favorite childhood Saturday morning cartoon character."

Leena chuckled.

"He had no plan, no destination, and all the time in the world to get there. Paul's travels took him across Europe, Asia, and Africa. It was while he was volunteering at an aid station relief camp in Eritrea, a country in the Horn of Africa, that he received some sad news."

"Oh no," Leena whispered.

Paul held up his hand and continued. "Eritrea, as you know, is bordered by Sudan in the west, Ethiopia in the south, and Djibouti in the southeast, with the northeastern and eastern coastlines butting up against the Red Sea. Although they continually deny it, the Eritrean government's human rights record is considered among the worst in the world. Its people live in constant fear, not only from their neighbors who would do them harm, but from their own government, which had proven time and time again that they did not have their citizen's best interests at heart."

"But, what of the sad news?" Leena enquired.

"I'm getting to that," Paul said. "Paul had been living out of a tent in the muddy field the relief workers called home. There were doctors, aid workers, and civilian volunteers from four different countries working in the field. Conditions were far from ideal, but he rose to the challenge. The people he worked with knew him as Paul Sanders, a man interested in helping. No one knew of his family's fortunes and he preferred it that way.

"Paul had surreptitiously routed some money from his private reserve to the aid station. It had come in handy to procure some much-needed medical supplies as well as blankets and heating oil for the winter season. He thought he had dropped completely off the grid. Then one day, a package was delivered addressed to a Mr. Paul Sanderson. It was marked URGENT. And just like that, his secret was a secret no longer."

Paul again leaned on the Lair's railing and looked away into the distance. "The only thing that moved faster than the cheetah or a wildfire across the plains was rumor and gossip. It did not take long for this new piece of news to spread across the camp and possibly beyond. Inside the package was a letter from the family retainer, Jonathan Simpson. It was frank and to the point, just like the man who wrote it. The letter read:

"Master Sanderson,

"I regret that I have to deliver this news to you in such an informal way as a letter, but my efforts to get in touch with you using modern communication techniques have proven difficult. It is with profound regret that I must inform you of the death of your parents.

"There was more, but he only skimmed the rest. The death of one's parents, while inevitable, was still a shock. Paul read the rest of the letter then re-read the entire thing two more times before he could take it all in.

"In his letter, Simpson related the details of his parents' death in a car accident. The officials had declared it a tragic accident, a blow out on a curvy road in the rain. Their deaths were deemed accidental and the case was quickly closed and filed. It seemed so strange, though. His parents were never ones to drive themselves anywhere. Usually, they had Simpson or someone on the staff chauffeur them wherever they needed to go. That they had perished in a car accident on one of the few nights they had bothered to drive themselves was too ironic for words. It made the pain of the situation all the more acute somehow. It was simply an accident. Tragic, but they happened. Case closed."

"Oh no," Leena said.

"Paul felt sad when he read the news, of course. They were his parents and he loved them, but he had never truly known them. At the end of the day, Robert and Anna Sanderson were little more than strangers to him. And that reality made the pain of their loss strangely unbearable to him."

"I...I don't know what to say, darling," Leena said, emotion welling up in her pretty face. "I know they weren't your parents, and yet..."

"And yet they were, or feel like they were. Yes, I know," Paul said. "The other envelope was sealed from an attorney's office. Before opening it, Paul knew it was about the will and his inheritance. As he suspected, they had left the lion's share of the estate and family holdings to him, save a few charitable contributions and bonus stipends for Simpson and the staff. He didn't care about the money. Not really. There was a substantial sum in his trust, which he had been using to fund his travels and help the camp with much-needed medical supplies on the sly. No, he didn't really care about his family's money, but he couldn't ignore how much good could be done with it, so he decided to put it to good use. He would use his family's fortune and their good name to make the world a better place. What better way to celebrate their lives and legacy, he decided."

He took a seat beside Leena. "The last item in the package was a small leather box. He, of course, recognized it immediately. It was his father's Rolex Submariner. His father had bought it just before he'd left on his travels. When Paul had related to them he was leaving college to see the world, his father barely registered any emotion, so enamored was he of the new toy on his left wrist.

"A note from Simpson was attached: *Your father wanted you to have this,* was all it said.

"Paul assumed that wasn't actually true, probably just Simpson trying to bring them together, as he tried so many times in the past. It hadn't worked when they lived in Metro City. It didn't work any better in the Horn of Africa. Or had it?"

Paul averted his gaze again, and let his thoughts wander into memory.

* * * * * *

ERITREA – EIGHT YEARS EARLIER

Instinctively, Paul put on the watch. He didn't know what else to do, despite feeling a little animosity toward the timepiece.

His thoughts raced across the desert and the sea and all the way back to the lush greenery of his home back in Metro City. He missed Simpson, the closest thing he had to a friend. He wondered how Simpson was faring now that the Sanderson's were not there. Would he have to find a new job? Paul hated the thought of his friend struggling to make ends meet.

The aid camp was expecting a supply drop in a few days. He would see if the couriers had a satellite phone so he could at least call and talk to Simpson, let him know he received the news and was sorry for his loss. Simpson had been closer to his parents than he was. Surely the news had devastated him. He also wanted to ask Simpson to stay on and take care of the house and estate. That home was as much Simpson's as his, maybe even more so. Paul wanted him to stay there. It seemed wrong somehow for Simpson not to be in that house.

With his secret out, Paul wondered if it was time to move on again. Now that the word was out on who he really was, things would no doubt change. He started making plans to leave. Surprisingly, at least to him, no one treated him any differently. He wasn't peppered with questions, even though he assumed the workers had many. Even a continent away, the Sanderson name was known and mostly respected.

Not even Judy Hess, who he worked with most often, treated him any different. He was glad and not a little relieved. Judy was a medical student with a heart of gold and a smile to match. She was on her way to becoming a brilliant doctor. She was smart, kind and caring, with a heart bigger than the continent they currently called home. She had opted to take a semester of her field studies in Eritrea. When she finished here, she would spend several months working in a Chicago emergency room. There were times Paul wondered which was the more dangerous of the two: Eritrea or Chicago. Neither was exactly safe as far as he was concerned. She assured him she had grown up in Chicago and had managed to turn out just fine. She had no worries about returning there to work.

In Eritrea, the locals already called her Dr. Judy. For a time, she tried to correct them and let them know she was not a doctor yet, but eventually she gave up and graciously accepted the nickname with gratitude and a smile.

Oh, that smile, Paul thought.

He and Judy had worked closely together since he arrived. That closeness developed into a blossoming romance, or at least the modern day equivalent of two ships passing in the night. They both knew making long-lasting relationships in the wild under less than ideal living circumstances was problematic at best, impossible at worst. One rainy night, while huddled together in a single sleeping bag for warmth while cold rainwater leaked into her tent, Paul and Judy made a plan. He was all for riding it out and seeing where things went, but she was more analytical. She wanted to define their relationship and where they thought they were going. He knew he would follow her into the gates of Hell and back if he had to. It was the closest thing to a true and honest relationship he had ever experienced, but neither of them were ready to call it love. Not yet.

They made a good couple. Paul was tall and lanky, his brown hair and pale skin uncommon for the region. He pulled a few strings for extra sunscreen as he sunburned easily and often, even on the cloudy days. Judy was three to four inches shorter than he was and her smooth brown skin and raven-black hair was a stark contrast to him. She often stood on tiptoe when they danced in her tent on those rare occasions when her transistor radio managed to pick up a signal or when they kissed goodnight.

She was brilliant. Once his true identity had been revealed, she quickly put two and two together and realized most of the money he had given them had not come from multiple anonymous donors like he had reported when he arrived, but from him personally. She thanked him when she figured it out and told him to get back to work, so he decided to stay just a little longer. She never asked him to use his money for anything else, but he offered what he could when it was needed.

Paul had been looking for something to help fill the emptiness in his soul. He wouldn't have believed it possible he would find himself in Africa helping Eritrea's needy and the forgotten, that he would find his life's calling, or that he would meet the woman of his dreams.

For the first time in a long time, Paul Sanderson was content. He was almost afraid to admit it, but he was maybe even a little bit happy.

He should have known better.

~ Chapter 5 ~

"It sounds idyllic, in a dirty, sweaty kind of way," Leena said, engrossed in the story so far. She couldn't wait to hear more.

"It was. For the first time in his life, Paul started to feel at home, at ease in his own skin. It wasn't to last. Disaster was just around the corner."

* * * * * *

ERITREA - EIGHT YEARS EARLIER

The next few weeks passed by without too much excitement.

Then the rains came.

A torrential downpour lasted four and a half days before there was a break in the storm. The break was short-lived before the next monsoon hit. One of the volunteers joked, "If you don't like the weather in Eritrea...give it a minute." It was an accurate depiction of the inconsistent weather patterns Paul had noticed since he arrived. Not only did they have to fear the warlords, poachers, and the wild animals, but the country itself seemed eager to kill them all.

Instead of cooling off the high temperatures, as it did back home, the rain washed away the meager crops they had been able to grow and flooded the valley. It also brought with it a thick humidity unlike any Paul had felt before. He did not think such a thing was possible, but the air was so heavy it was like walking through a bowl of molasses.

The humidity also brought another surprise—mosquitoes the size of walnuts.

Despite their best efforts to keep the blood-sucking insects at bay, the mosquitoes were everywhere. All of the locals as well as the aid workers required inoculations against Malaria, the West Nile Virus, Dengue Fever, Yellow Fever, Elephantiasis, and those were just the big ones. There remained any number of infections that could arise, or stomach troubles for anyone who took a drink from the contaminated water supply. The team acted quickly and was able to get everyone vaccinated efficiently. There were no major outbreaks—just a few cases of fever and vomiting—but they passed quickly under the expert touch of Dr. Judy and her team.

Disaster was averted, but between the flood and the aftermath, their supplies were sorely depleted. As soon as he could get his hands on a sat-phone, he would see what he could do to grease the wheels on that delayed supply run.

A few days later, the supplies finally arrived.

Paul unloaded some long overdue medical supplies the Red Cross had promised them weeks earlier. The Red Cross Jeep had arrived just ahead of the box truck. Both of them were loaded with much-needed items like insulin, antibiotics, water purification tablets, blankets, food, coloring books, batteries, IV fluids, blood, and more.

The shipment was like a gift from the heavens.

"This is the last of them?" Judy asked as Paul stacked a box inside the supply tent.

"The very last one," he said with a tired smile. He wiped the sweat from his forehead. "We picked that truck clean."

"Thanks for your help, Paul."

"My pleasure," he said as he walked up behind her and wrapped his sweaty arms around her diminutive frame.

She giggled as he nuzzled the back of her neck, the soft whiskers of his cheek tickling her skin. "Time and place, Mr. Sanderson," she said. Like most, she told him it had taken her a long time to get used to referring to him as Paul Sanderson after thinking of him as Paul Sanders for so long. Some still hadn't gotten used to it, not that he minded one way or another.

"In that case, let's just get back there and inoculate as many of the children as we can today. What do you say, Dr. Judy?"

She smiled. "You're on, Nurse Sanderson."

Each carrying a box of medical supplies, they walked toward the large tented area that served as the field hospital.

Judy playfully nudged him. "You've never been very open to talking about yourself, Paul," she started.

Uh oh.

"Why are you here?" she asked, and he breathed a sigh of relief. "You're part of the Sanderson Empire. You could have anything you want. Be anywhere you want. Why are you here?"

"Here is exactly where I want to be, Judy," he said and meant it. "I want to help. That's all."

The field hospital was filled with the sick and the starving. Many of their patients had never even heard the word "doctor" before meeting Judy. For others, this was the only place they could get a hot meal or a new blanket to sleep under. The relief camp fulfilled many roles for the locals. The kids were crazy for the coloring and storybooks, and the adults were happy to accept the donated clothing that was handed out. Others were simply grateful there was someone they could talk to, someone who cared and listened.

The Horn of Africa's weather swung from oppressively hot to frigid without warning, sometimes in the same day—freeze in the morning and roast by the afternoon. No wonder most of them were unhealthy.

The heat was more cruel than usual of late and Paul constantly had to wipe away the sweat. Water was their most valuable resource during the hot seasons. Dehydration could be lethal on the plains.

The aid station had eight volunteers. Paul and Judy worked the hospital tent along with Doctors Jay Perry and Pamela Requard. Dr. Perry was from California and part of Doctors Without Borders, and Dr. Requard was from London and on loan from Doctors Unlimited, a group based out of the UK. Samantha Winters, Marcus Rawston, and Wayne Ash were volunteers who had joined a program at their college in Athens, Georgia. They were short timers who would only be there a month before they were rotated out and new classmates of theirs flown in. In addition to helping, for which they earned college credits, they also studied the local customs for a paper they would write on life in Eritrea. The last member of the staff was Tyler Hawkins, a pilot from the United States. Hawkins had been a major in the air force before retiring and opening his own charter business.

Rumor had it he was a fifth-generation flyer and his father, uncle, grandfather, great grandfather, and great-great grandfather were all bona-fide air aces. His Midwest drawl gave away his origins immediately, but he was a jovial sort, always laughing or telling a joke. Yet once he was in the helicopter that had been loaned out to them for emergency runs and to keep a bird's eye view on the surroundings, he was all business. The helicopter was also their escape craft in case one of the local warlords paid too close attention to what they were doing.

All of the bribes had been paid off, but warlords and unscrupulous government officials were not always known for sticking to their word. If there was trouble, Hawkins could have them airborne and away from the aid station within minutes if need be.

With a supply run having arrived, the helicopter flew cover for the vehicles coming into camp and heading back out. The round trip normally took about an hour, give or take. They weren't expecting to need the chopper during that window.

A few of the locals also helped out around camp. Some swept while others moved boxes, cooked, washed dishes or clothes, and other helpful things. None of it was necessary or required, of course, but they were a proud people and wanted to help anyway they could. Judy could not insult them by sending them away.

"It's not that I'm not grateful," Judy said as she and Paul put down their boxes in the field hospital and started unloading them. The other volunteers performed similar work with the rest of the supplies that needed immediate restocking.

"You've given us money, which has given us food and medicine..." she continued.

"Then what is it? I'm starting to get that bad feeling I get right before I'm shown the door," Paul said, only half joking.

She stroked his cheek, her soft fingers warm against his skin, almost electric. "I just think you could help us better by..."

Paul kissed her before she could say anything more. It was meant as a distraction, but the truth was, he had wanted to kiss her all day.

Judy surrendered and fell into him, each clutching onto each other in the supply corner.

Paul heard a couple of the local children snicker.

"I'm not going anywhere," he said once they came up for air.

"I should hope not," Judy said.

"Then what were you going to say?"

She barked a laugh. "I'm certainly not going to tell you now."

"Why not?" Paul said, feigning hurt feelings.

She pursed her lips and shot him a dirty look.

"I think the lady doth protest too much, how about you?" Paul asked one of the kids standing nearby, giving the child a silly look.

The kid giggled.

"Oh, shut up and get back to work or you're fired," Judy said with a giggle of her own.

"Yes, ma'am," Paul said with a laugh.

Unpacking and organizing the supplies went faster than he'd expected. He was about to ask her what else needed to be done when he heard a noise. He stepped out of the tent into the hot, humid air. The sound was familiar. There were vehicles approaching. He couldn't see them yet, but a dust cloud was kicked off to their south, the same way the shipment had come from. South was the only secure route in or out of the area. The other roads were either booby trapped or guarded by local warlords.

A moment later, Judy joined him outside.

"Are we expecting another delivery today?" Paul asked, fearing the answer.

"Not that I know of," she said. She had a pair of binoculars in her hand. She gazed out at the incoming caravan. "Oh no."

"What? Who is it?" Paul asked. "One of the warlords?"

"Worse."

She handed him the binoculars and he took a look himself. He saw a flotilla of army vehicles approaching, each one jam-packed with armed soldiers and all of them heading straight toward the camp.

"That can't be good," he said.

"It's not," Judy said. "We're in trouble. That's General Abdelkrim."

"Who's he?"

"A ruthless man who fancies himself the dictator of Eritrea. They call him the Cobra."

Paul's jaw clenched tight.

He recognized *that* name.

Everyone in Eritrea knew it and feared it.

"You're right," he said. "We're in big trouble."

~ Chapter 6 ~

Paul Sanderson helplessly watched as the first of the general's men arrived.

Although he had never had the privilege of meeting General Abdelkrim in person, a fact for which he was eternally grateful, he'd heard stories about the self-proclaimed *Absolute Ruler of Eritrea*, who was also known as the Cobra because of the cobra-shaped scar over his right eye.

General Kaseem Abdelkrim was a bad man, worse than the warlords who were rumored to work for him unless an international television news crew was close by, then, he would fly the flag and tell sad stories of savages combing the countryside and waging war on Eritrea's poor citizenry. Once the cameras were gone, he was happy to see those citizens gone.

The Cobra believed anyone too poor or sickly to work for him did not deserve to live. Those who stood against him were labeled radicals and arrested or shot on sight. The general's enemies did not survive long enough to become a major threat.

The vehicles tore through the camp, kicking up plumes of dust into the air. The natives ran for cover, hoping to get away before the general's men saw them. As much as they came to trust the Americans who brought them food, medicine, and clothing, Paul knew they did not believe any of them were strong enough to stand up to the butcher of Eritrea.

General Abdelkrim stood in the lead car, his teeth gleaming white in the bright sun. He was tall, easily standing seven feet, with long black hair that whipped around in the breeze kicked up by the vehicles bouncing on the uneven ground and sending dirt into the air. The general was decked out in full military fashion with his gray uniform tailored and adorned with medals displaying his militaristic rank and moral superiority, some of it earned and some of it, by all reports, appropriated. Bright red epaulets stood out like bloody bars against the gray fabric on his shoulder. His face was dark and tanned as leather from many long days in the sun without protection. Even then, Paul noticed the general did not wear a hat to shade his face.

The man's most interesting feature was the facial tattoo that gave him his frightening sobriquet—the Cobra. The inky creature's mouth began above the general's right eyebrow and the body wound its way down his face to a place on his cheek where the tail ended in a point. The cobra tattoo rested just above the black goatee beard that was beginning to show a few strands of white in its bushy whiskers.

In Eritrea, everyone knew to fear the Cobra. To lay eyes upon the general and his tattoo was tantamount to a death sentence. The locals knew to avert their eyes lest the evil one's gaze fell upon them.

The newcomers were not as well trained.

Paul's first thought was the man looked like a villain right out of an 80s straight-to-video action movie, except this guy was truly dangerous and there was no super-powered hero around to stand against him. In Eritrea, the bad guy had won and there was no one left to make things right.

The general's men were dressed more casually than their leader, but no less dangerous. Each of them, including their boss, wore a gun belt and each had a machete sheathed and strapped to their leg. These men meant business.

Paul and Judy stepped between the new arrivals and the hospital tent.

General Abdelkrim exited his vehicle and slowly approached the couple. He smiled, but there was no joy in his toothy grin, only menace. He was dangerous and powerful, and it was clear he wanted to make sure they knew it. A soft chuckle escaped his lips as he approached.

Paul tried to position himself in front of Judy, but she would not allow him to protect her. She closed the gap between herself and the killer in the military garb.

"Ah...Dr. Judy...so good to see you again," he said playfully, like a cat toying with its favorite mouse before the ringing of the dinner bell.

"What are..." Judy started, but evidently reined her temper back in. Paul knew she needed to stay on the general's good side if they were to have any hope of getting out of this mess alive. "What can we do for you, General?"

"You have been warned before about setting up your camp in this province, have you not? This is a dangerous area. There are many" —his smile widened— "predators out here in the wild."

"Your concern for our well-being is appreciated, General," Judy said.

"Of course, Dr. As a duly elected representative of Eritrea, the safety of my people and guests to our country like yourself is, of course, our utmost concern."

Duly elected? Paul thought. *That's a laugh.*

Judy screwed on her best smile, one Paul knew as a fake. "You're too kind, sir."

"We do not condone your presence here, Dr," Abdelkrim said. "It would be best if you and your—what do you American's call them again?—Ah yes, 'bleeding hearts' were to vacate the area immediately."

"There are a lot of sick people here," Judy said.

"And I assure you we will take good care of them. Thank you for bringing this much-needed medicine to our people. My men and I will make certain it is distributed to our people forthwith. You have my guarantee."

"You have no right to stop us," she said, raising her voice. "We're a legally-sanctioned international aid agency. We are here only to help feed and medicate your sick and starving. We have no interest in your stupid border wars."

"You seem to be under the misguided notion I am offering you a choice, Dr. I assure you, I am not, so I ask you one final time—Are you leaving? Yes or no?"

"No."

Without another word, Abdelkrim raised his left arm.

The soldiers surrounding him opened fire.

Surprised by the suddenness of the attack, Judy flailed backward under the intense gunfire, but there was nowhere to go.

Paul could only watch in horror as her body was shredded to pieces by the barrage of bullets fired by the soldiers.

The lifeless corpse that fell to the ground was no longer Judy Hess.

Dr Judy was gone.

Something primal clawed its way up from deep inside Paul Sanderson and escaped as a scream that would have made even the Lord of Hades stand up and pay attention. Even the general and his men were clearly taken aback at the savage cry that erupted from such a slender man.

Paul ran over to Judy's body. Tears streamed down his face as he pulled her close. With chaos exploding all around him, Paul Sanderson cradled the body of the woman he loved—yes, damn it, he *loved* her—and shouted to the heavens even though he doubted anyone was listening.

General Abdelkrim walked toward them like a man out for a leisurely stroll, but like the monster he was, chuckled at the mayhem he had wrought as if the chaos pleased him.

He stopped and looked down at the dead woman and her crying suitor. He watched with seeming amusement as Paul tried to protect the lifeless corpse that had once been the camp doctor.

Abdelkrim chuckled. "You're wasting your time, American," he said, his voice firm but calm. "Her life was forfeit the moment she dared defy me."

Paul looked up at General Abdelkrim. Hatred burned in his soul.

"You want to see defiance?" Paul said. "I'll show you defiance."

It was an empty threat. They both must have known that. Paul was vastly outnumbered and outgunned.

"All who disobey me will meet the same fate," General Abdelkrim said as he began pacing back and forth in front of Paul. "You cannot defy me."

Paul shot him a dirty look, but said nothing.

With a wave of his fingers, the general ordered one of the soldiers to pull Paul to his feet.

"What is your name, boy?" the general asked.

Paul shot daggers at the man, but stayed silent, his jaw clenched.

The general stopped pacing and looked him in the eyes. "You do not want to make me ask you twice," the general said, an eyebrow arched skyward.

"P...P...Paul," he said over quivering lips.

"Excellent, P...P...Paul," the general said. "Who is in charge here?"

Paul looked down at Judy, blind rage clutching at his chest. "She was."

"Wrong answer," Abdelkrim said.

The soldier punched Paul in the stomach, doubling him over and sending him crashing to his knees and coughing to try and catch his breath.

The general nodded and the soldier jerked his prisoner back to his feet.

Abdelkrim leaned in close so Paul could plainly hear him. "*I* am in charge here," the general whispered.

Something snapped within. Moving on pure rage, Paul jammed his elbow into the nose of the guard standing behind him. Bone and cartilage shattered on impact and pushed upward into the man's brain.

Like Judy, he was dead before he hit the ground.

The attack was as swift as it was sudden, catching everyone off guard.

"You sonuva..." Paul snarled at the general.

Fury spurred him on and Paul leapt at General Abdelkrim, teeth bared and hands clenched into claws. He grabbed the general by the jacket collar and pulled him close. Paul cocked his fist, but he wasn't fast enough.

General Abdelkrim moved faster. "Infidel!" he shouted as a powerful backhand sent Paul flying backward.

Paul landed face first in the African dust, blood pouring from his split lip. Before he could sit up, the general barked an order to his men.

"Leave no one standing!" he shouted.

The soldiers unleashed a full volley, killing every man, woman, and child in the camp. Some fled, running, trying to get to safety, while others attempted to hide from the soldiers. Gunfire bombarded the tents and quickly ripped them to shreds. The medicine and supplies were ignited, taking only a moment to flare into a raging inferno.

All was lost.

* * * * * *

"This is terrible," Leena said, her voice tinged with sadness. "I never knew...how horrible...Judy..."

"Yes," Paul replied. A tear formed in the corner of one eye, Leena noted.

Clearly, the pain was still very evident, even though it was a life *this* Paul Sanderson never actually lived. None of this pain he was currently feeling, would no doubt forever feel, was real. And yet...

"Yes," Paul repeated, getting a hold of himself. "It was horrible. But this was just the beginning."

"Go on," Leena said, "if you're still able and willing."

Paul smiled and acquiesced. "Of the eight foreign volunteers, only Paul and Major Tyler Hawkins had been spared. Paul found out later the pilot had been out on a run despite the horrendous conditions. That run had saved the pilot's life."

He paused for a moment. Leena waited.

"Go on," she ultimately said.

~ Chapter 7 ~

ERITREA - EIGHT YEARS EARLIER

Paul could not explain why he still lived. The only reason he could think of was to offer entertainment to the general while they tortured him. Paul was not ready to prolong his agony. He pushed himself onto his knees, his vision blurred in one eye. Through the haze, he focused on General Abdelkrim, who proudly stood tall, laughing at the massacre he ordered.

"You..." Paul started.

There was no time to finish that thought as the soldier standing nearest to him brought down the butt of his rifle. The last thing Paul saw before the lights went out was the stock heading straight toward his face.

Then intense pain followed by nothing but darkness.

* * * * * *

Wake up, Paul! Paul thought he heard.

He awoke with the worst case of dry mouth in history.

You can't afford to be late for school!

Every inch of him hurt. His face felt as though it had been scrubbed with coarse sandpaper and even moving anything at all was a challenge. It took some doing, but with some effort, he was able to get his hands from beneath himself and pushed. He lifted himself just enough to roll over so he stared up into a bright, cloudless sky.

Above him, the scorching sun beat down on him so brightly it hurt to open his eyes. He shielded his vision with his hands, but that oppressive brightness was everywhere and with it came the desert heat. No humidity this time, just an all-penetrating heat. Drenched in sweat and blood, his clothes stuck to him along with the clinging sand as it dug into his reddened, blistered skin.

All he wanted to do was close his eyes and sleep, but even his exhausted mind knew that was a bad idea.

Five more minutes! Paul thought.

No! Get up! Get moving! a voice screamed at him.

It wasn't until he felt the metal of his watch's Oyster bracelet burning his skin that he realized the voice belonged to his father. Curious, he wondered why now, of all times, he heard the man so clearly. Until recently, he had not given him much thought—even his mother—yet, still, they were never far from his mind since Simpson's letter arrived back at the camp. Never far no matter how hard he tried to push them into a forgotten corner of his mind.

Their death seemed a lifetime ago now.

He pulled off the watch, undamaged and unmarked, and shoved it into his pants pocket, surprised the animals that had left him for dead hadn't stolen it. Surely, they would have recognized its monetary value.

Get up, young man!

He wiped at the dried blood on his nose, mouth, chin, and cheek. Based on how dry it was and that he was no longer sweating a great deal, Paul realized two things very quickly. He was dehydrated and the general's men had dragged him far into the desert and left him there to die. He needed water quickly, but somehow he suspected neither General Abdelkrim nor his men had left him a bottle of water nearby. Finding a local supply was a long shot at best. Most of the locals came to them at the aid camp for water and food.

Move!

"Well, here's another fine mess," Paul croaked over parched lips and tried to laugh, but his raw, scratchy throat refused to cooperate.

He couldn't laugh.

This is no time for levity, son.

He couldn't cry.

No crying. Sanderson men don't show emotion, son.

He could barely get up off the biting hot sand, but with effort, he was finally able to stand without falling back down. It was a small victory, but he would take it.

He did not recognize the surroundings, although there weren't many landmarks to choose from. In every direction he looked there was nothing but sand, sand and even more sand. To his left lay untold rolling dunes. To his right and before him was a flatter, sandy expanse. He couldn't be sure exactly where he was or how long he had been out here unconscious in the heat. One thing was certain: he would not survive if he stayed put. There was no one coming to save him. He would be surprised if anyone was actually looking for him.

His options were limited, if he had any at all.

He picked a direction—dead ahead—and forced himself to take a step, one foot in front of the other.

Then another step.

Then another.

And another.

Before long, he was walking again.

Of course, he had no idea where he was going, but he was soon working a decent pace, considering his injuries.

Paul continued onward on unsteady legs. His head spun, his vision blurred, and he heard his heartbeat thunder in his ears, but he refused to give up so kept trudging through the sand in search of safe harbor.

As the temperature rose, Paul shed his shirt and wrapped it around his head in an effort to keep his brain from boiling. He hoped it would quell the unnerving feeling he was about to pass out.

It didn't.

With his shirt torn and hanging over his head like a makeshift hat, the bedraggled, injured, and thirsty young man continued onward, praying the sun would soon set.

Eventually, he got his wish as the sky turned from bright, white hot to beautiful mixtures of red, yellow, and orange. If not for the fact he was only a stone's throw away from death, he would have thought the sunset sky was beautiful. Enchanting even. He and Judy had sat together, holding hands, as they watched many a sunset in their brief time together. The thought of his lost love brought a sudden pain within, but it also gave him the strength to go on; his anger and hatred toward Abdelkrim fueled his very limbs.

Paul stomped ungainly across the desert for a day, maybe two, moving like a zombie out of a movie. He tried to sleep during the hottest times of the day and walk during the cooler nights. But with no water or food, he could only go on that way for so long.

As far as the eye could see, there was a vast emptiness. As his mind cleared, Paul felt certain he had walked into the Danakil Depression region of Eritrea, many miles from the aid camp. Of course, that was all conjecture. One thing was certain: he could not hold out much longer under his current conditions without finding help or water. Since he knew there was no help coming, he accepted his inevitable demise. He knew this was the end.

Paul collapsed, face down in the dust.

Get up, young man!

"Father..." he croaked over cracked lips.

I'm sorry, son, but you know how busy I am with work.

"Fa...ther..."

His muscles felt like lead, too heavy to lift.

He was exhausted, dehydrated, and ready to die.

Lying face down in the desert, Paul Sanderson surrendered.

He closed his eyes.

What would Father think? was his last thought before darkness claimed him.

* * * * * *

"Oh my," was all Leena could say upon hearing this latest part of the story. "It's hard to see how anyone could have survived such an ordeal."

"He very nearly didn't," Paul replied. "If it hadn't been for Sam."

"Sam?"

"A native of the region. His real name was unpronounceable. 'Sam' seemed to fit—the name was from another of Paul's favorite Saturday morning cartoons—and he found the appellation amusing, I think. But...let me continue, Leena."

* * * * * *

ERITREA – EIGHT YEARS EARLIER

Delirious, Paul Sanderson talked to his father.

"Why did you leave me?" Paul croaked.

You know how busy I am with work, son, he heard his father say.

In his delirium, Paul thought he saw a native approaching him. As the stranger neared, his thoughts clarified slightly, and the voice of his father disappeared.

The native was one of the Tigrinya people. Before traveling to the country, Paul had done some research on the place and its people. He knew the Tigrinya were honest farmers and religious men who lived in small encampments scattered across the desert where they fought the harsh conditions to grow their crops. It was not an easy existence, but the Tigrinya were not afraid of hard work and they were sadly all too accustomed to the harsh realities of life. Their people had been forced out of their homeland and persecuted. Though they were few in number, the Tigrinya were a proud people with a long, rich history. They had adapted to survive in the inhospitable desert, to push back against the elements until the land bent to their will and their crops flourished.

* * * * * *

The native was covered from head to toe, outfitted in loose wrappings to protect him from the sun's brutal rays and to help keep him as close to comfortable as a man could get under the blazing white-hot desert sun.

When he discovered the man lying in the desert, uncovered and without provisions, the native feared the worst. Despite whatever circumstances had brought him there, the white man was not the first person to be found lying face down in the desert sands while the winds sandblasted the skin from his sun-bleached bones. It was a truly terrible way to die: slow and painful.

Desert life was hazardous. It was the enemy that had to be beaten back by those who chose to live in such harsh surroundings. Every single day.

The newcomer knelt beside the stranger's unconscious body and felt for a pulse. He was surprised to find the sunburned young man was still alive, albeit barely. Another hour exposed to the elements and he surely would have died.

The native was more than twice Paul's age, but he still worked the land and his muscles were strong. With ease, he hefted the unconscious man over his shoulder and headed for his camp, his crops neglected in favor of saving a stranger's life.

* * * * * *

Paul awoke with a start—and a pounding headache.

He lay on a small, makeshift cot, much like the ones they used at the hospital at the aid station. A thin blanket covered him, soft to the touch. On top of it lay a dusty, dirt-clotted furry blanket made from some sort of animal hide. Paul tried not to think about the poor animal that had once owned this fur.

Without getting up, he looked around the tent, pain stabbing through his eyes with each movement.

The room was small and dark, with packed sand making up the floor. He immediately recognized the wall as being made of thick canvas—a large family-sized tent. They had used the same type of tents at the aid station.

Have I somehow made it back to camp? he wondered as he closed his eyes against the pain.

Thoughts of the camp brought back flashes of memory. Images of Judy Hess swam before him, smiling as she ran through a field of tall green grass without so much as a care in the world. She smiled at him as she looked back over her shoulder to see if he was following her. He was. Paul would have followed her to the ends of the Earth.

He would follow her to Hell and back.

In fact, he had.

Judy smiled at him, but soon her smile faded.

Suddenly, a large *CRACK!* tore through the night.

A gunshot!

Paul leapt to his feet just as the tent flap opened.

"Ah! There you are," General Abdelkrim said as he pointed his pistol at him. "Time to die, American!"

I'm sorry, son, but you know how busy I am with work. His father's words continued to haunt him.

Paul screamed in defiance.

Then woke up.

Again.

The realization he had dozed back off and dreamed the general had found him hit him like a concrete block to the chest. He couldn't sit up, couldn't catch his breath. Panic started to set in.

Once he realized it was all a dream, his heart rate slowly dropped back to its normal rhythm. His parents were dead. Judy was dead. They were all dead. He knew that. He also knew there was nothing he could do to change that fact. For reasons he could not understand, Paul Sanderson had been spared the fate of his companions. He did not know why. All he knew was he had no idea how to get justice for his slain friends.

At least not yet.

He looked around the tent, wondering if that had been a dream as well.

It hadn't been.

There were very few personal items he could see. There was a framed photo of a family sitting on a wooden box next to a candle that softly flickered. His father's wristwatch also sat atop the box. He couldn't be sure, but it appeared undamaged. Strings draped down from the top of the tent and curled back up to the opposite side. Paul assumed they were clotheslines as stray pieces of cloth hung from some of them. Two clay pots sat on opposite corners of the room, weighing down the edges of the thick rug that sat atop the sandy floor. The cot held down the opposite side.

Paul reached out and touched the canvas nearest to the bed. There was something hard on the other side. From the texture and the coolness of its touch, he assumed it was a rock face, which put him near the mountains.

He was surprised he had made it that far.

I couldn't have without help, he decided.

Paul sat up; the room began to spin. "Ooooh...maybe not the best idea," he muttered through gritted teeth.

"You are feeling recovered, yes?" a strange voice called from the opposite side of the tent. It was heavily accented, but it was English.

Paul started and quickly sat down. He'd assumed he was alone since he hadn't seen anyone else in the room.

With the flaps closed, the tent was dark, so it took a moment for his eyes to adjust to the dim light from the lone candle flickering in the corner.

"You are feeling recovered, yes?" the man repeated.

"I...I think so," Paul said softly, his voice and throat extremely dry. It was only partly true. Every inch of him hurt, but at least he no longer felt like he was going to pass out. "Did you get the number of the freight train that ran over me?" he said, trying to be funny.

"Freight train?" the man asked, puzzled. "There is no train tracks in my desert."

"Never mind," Paul said and waved the comment away. He hurt too much to laugh.

The man sat cross-legged on the carpet, presumably the one who had saved his life. He was much older than Paul, but he did not look frail. The man was clearly native to the Bihére-Tigrinya because he wore the traditional garb of the region. He was covered in robes, with only his face and head uncovered inside the tent. Strips of cloth were wrapped around his hands like bandages. The robes were stained and worn, which made Paul assume this man was a farmer, used to the daily grind of hard, manual labor.

"Who are you?" Paul asked.

"I am..." And he proceeded to rattle off a string of consonants and vowels that should never stand next to one another.

"Uh huh," Paul said. "I don't think I'm going to be able to remember that, much less pronounce it correctly."

"It is not a difficult name."

"Easy for you to say."

"Yes," the native said, chuckling at his new friend's discomfort.

"How about 'Sam'? Can I call you Sam? Sam's a good name. I like Sam."

The native thought it over and nodded, smiling as he did so. He appeared to find the appellation amusing and Paul was glad because there was no way he would ever be able to pronounce the farmer's real name. Not in this lifetime.

"Thank you," Paul said weakly as the tent began to spin around him. Nausea bubbled within his gut. He didn't throw up. There was nothing *to* throw up.

"You should rest, my friend," Sam said. "We can talk later."

"Paul," he offered by way of introduction as he lay back down on the cot. "That's my name. I'm Paul. Paul Sanderson."

Sam smiled. "We shall talk after you are rested and healed, friend Paul. You will be safe here. You have my solemn word."

"Thank you," Paul said.

Sam nodded.

Paul smiled as he watched Sam open a flap in the tent to another section of tent beyond. He thought he saw children moving about, but wondered why anyone in their right mind would bring a child, much less more than one, into such inhospitable terrain.

Before he could dwell on it further, Paul drifted off into peaceful sleep.

Once again, he dreamed of his father.

~ Chapter 8 ~

Paul had no idea how long he had been there.

Everything from the attack on the aid camp to finding himself face down in the desert to waking up in Sam's home began to merge together into one long, fever-induced nightmare. Although he was too incoherent to tell his new friend, Paul had worked with Judy and the staff at the aid camp long enough to recognize the effects of heatstroke, though he often heard the natives in this region call it sunstroke. The hospital had treated several cases while he was there and it was a very serious, often life-threatening condition. If your body temperature reached a certain level, you were dead. A one-hundred-and-four-degree temperature kicked off heatstroke. Although he did not have a thermometer handy, Paul suspected he had passed one-oh-four and was still climbing.

He had been alone in the desert, unprotected and without hydration for so long that his body had begun to shut down.

Paul mentally ticked off the symptoms in his head. Throbbing headache? *Check.* Dizziness and light-headedness? *Check and check.* Lack of sweating despite the heat? *Check again.* Red, hot, and/or dry skin? *My arms remind me of the last lobster I ate.* Muscle weakness or cramps? *Batting a thousand.* Nausea and vomiting? *Definitely check.* Rapid heartbeat, either strong or weak? *My thumper's beating like it's part of a* The Who *song.* Rapid, shallow breathing? *Yes, but improving. Good news there.* Confusion, disorientation, or staggering? *Yes, yes, and who can stand up?* Seizures? *Not yet. No check for you.* Unconsciousness? *Sleep. Blessed sleep. See? Darn near cured already.*

Paul couldn't tell for sure how long he'd tossed and turned in his fevered dream state, but he remembered the dreams. He was back in Metro City at the Sanderson home. His parents were getting ready for some gala event they were always running off to and completely ignored him.

They look so young, Paul thought as he sat on the floor and watched them make preparations to leave. Simpson was bringing the car around and all seemed normal.

Until he looked down and saw his adult hands. He wasn't a little kid, but that's what they saw when they looked at him. To them he was just a little child, a burden always under foot.

This has to be a dream.

"What time will you be home?" Paul asked. His voice sounded strange, the pitch higher than what he was used to hearing.

"We'll be late, son," Father said. "You'll already be asleep when we get home."

"Can I stay up and wait for you?"

His father shook his head in disappointment. "I'm afraid not. You have to learn how to stick to your schedule and do as you're told, Paul. You'll never make it in life without structure, son."

"Oh, for Heaven's sake, Robert," Paul's mother said. "He's still a long way from being ready to take over the company. Isn't that right, dear?"

"You coddle the boy too much, Anna," his father said as if Paul was no longer in the room. "Sanderson men have to be strong. The boy needs discipline. He needs to grow up."

"Like you did? That's what you really mean, isn't it? You want Paul to be cold and distant like you!"

"The boy could do worse than to be like me."

"The way your father made you be like him?"

"I am nothing like my father!"

"Have you considered Paul might never be anything like his father?"

Before Robert Sanderson could respond, Paul woke up.

Once again he found himself in the shade of the tent near the cool rocks.

"Where am I?"

"You are safe," Sam said from his usual spot across the tent where he sat silently.

Sam had given him water, shelter, and medication that had helped stave off the fever, but reducing it was another matter. Paul heard his heart pounding in his ears like the big bass drum that crazy Taylor kid down the street used to play in the school's marching band. He hated that instrument then. He hated the pounding in his head now.

"Stay calm," Sam's voice told him through the haze that was probably just his blurred vision than actually something floating in the air. Sam and a woman Paul assumed was his wife kept him cooled off with a wet washcloth on his forehead and cool wet towels beneath his armpits, groin, neck, and back. A salve had been applied to his burns and a bitter tasting root had been put under his tongue. Sam called it a powerful medicine.

Paul didn't believe him, but true or not, it helped him somehow manage to sleep.

This time, he did not remember dreaming.

* * * * * *

Two days later, Paul awoke a new man.

The fever had broken during the night and his body began to sweat again. He was still lightheaded and not so nimble on his feet, but he could stand and could walk, so that was considered a vast improvement. The urge to vomit was gone as well. The headache remained, but it was tolerable.

Not only had Sam saved his life, but had welcomed him into his home as if he was a brother or, at least, a close relative. While he recuperated, Paul slept on a cot in the tent while Sam and his family slept in another alongside it. There were three tents in all that made up Sam's dwelling, each a heavy canvas bag and all stitched together like rooms that could be accessed without going outside to brave the elements. Sam and his wife made one of the tents their bedroom while their three daughters shared another tent. Paul slept in the third, a parlor for welcoming visitors or just a sitting room for the family on story nights when Sam would regale them all with tales of stalwart heroes and vile villains, of monsters and quests, and prophecy yet unfulilled.

Paul enjoyed listening to Sam weave his tall tales for the children, who giggled and played along as his stories pulled them into the narrative. Paul had ascertained Sam and his family had been taught English at another aid station and associated school some time back, and enjoyed speaking in that language. Paul felt the man was a natural born storyteller with an exquisite imagination. With his deep, husky voice, Paul figured his new friend could make a killing as a Hollywood voice actor, but he was also certain Sam would never leave this desert.

Sam was everything Paul thought a good father should be. He laughed and played with his children, held them close when thunder and lightning split their peaceful night's dreams. The family took meals together and Sam never once foisted his children off on anyone. Paul envied Sam's girls, who he had nicknamed Huey, Lewey, and Dewey because he butchered their real names as well.

They thought the nicknames were hilarious and gave him one of his own—Sandman, a combination of his last name and where their father had found him.

The kitchen and eating area were inside the rock against which the tents had been pitched. Sam had spent many days and nights carving away at the rock so his family could have the protection of a roof over their head not made of flimsy cloth. The cooking stove warmed the rocks, which in turn warmed the tents.

The food that Sam's wife, Mala—the only one whose name he could even remotely pronounce correctly—prepared was heavenly. Though they didn't have a lot, she made sure that meals consisted of at least two vegetables and one meat, poultry or pork, food so spicy Paul was certain he had burned out his sinuses on the second meal. But they were tasty, so very tasty.

It was a tight squeeze in their ramshackle home of rock, dirt and cloth, but Sam had taken Paul in without question. He had stanched his wounds, fed him and gave him access to what little water they had. This was not the first time he had seen such compassion and generosity in this part of the world. Sam was a good man.

Judy would have liked him, Paul decided.

Since Paul Sanderson found himself in this small but comfortable home, the days and weeks began to roll one into the other. He spent his time playing with the girls, who taught him a few new board games. When he noticed they had a deck of cards, Paul reciprocated by teaching the girls and their parents how to play Go Fish and Gin Rummy. He was not surprised to learn Sam already knew how to play Poker and was quite adept at the game. Paul thought briefly about asking him where he had learned to play with such skill before realizing it must have been at the same aid camp where he and his family had learned English so well.

Paul wanted to ask Sam how long they had been there living in their tents, but instead chose to ask how long it had been since Sam found him.

"Fate has an odd way of placing us where we need to be," Sam only said.

"Uh huh," Paul replied, puzzled by such an odd answer. Added to that, he thought Sam sounded like a fortune cookie.

In the desert, there was night and day, and one day was virtually the same as the next until Paul could no longer differentiate between them. Had he been there a week or a month? Honestly, he could not say.

One morning he awoke to the sweetest aroma on Earth.

Coffee.

Mala was in the kitchen, roasting green coffee beans in a pan over an open flame. The smell was glorious. Paul asked her what she was doing, but Sam quickly escorted him to the table where his daughters were waiting. It had been so long since Paul had tasted coffee. It was one of his vices. Even in the desert heat, he would have settled for a bad cup just to enjoy that rich, hearty, caffeinated goodness.

With great care, Mala ground the beans and boiled the water while the rest of the family and their guest watched the process. Mala made a show of each step, with her husband, and his divine voice, narrating the entire performance as though it was a night at the theater. Once the beans were sufficiently roasted, she passed the steaming pot in front of each of them, starting with Sam, then her children, and finally to Paul, allowing each of them the opportunity to inhale the aroma.

The beans were then added to the Jebena to boil then cooled, then boiled again. She repeated the process until the coffee was perfected.

Once she was finished creating her delicacy, Mala brought the coffee to the table where she poured the liquid into small ceramic cups with no handles that already contained a small amount of sugar and powdered milk. The sweet aroma filled the tent. Paul would later learn this type of coffee ceremony was a common ritual amongst the Eritrean people.

After the first sip, they each took turns complimenting Mala on the fine pot of coffee she had prepared. Mala, as gracious as always, accepted the compliments and poured a second cup while Sam passed out small wood-fired biscuits to accompany the coffee.

Paul felt honored to have been allowed to partake of such a personal, family moment, and he told Sam and Mala so.

"The honor of sharing our home and coffee is ours," Mala said with a genuine smile.

Sam simply nodded in agreement with his wife.

After the coffee was passed around the table and everyone was enjoying it, Sam and Paul talked as best they could. Each of them knew only a little of the other's language. Although Sam's grasp of English was excellent, it was nevertheless still limited in its capability but far exceeded Paul's modest grasp of the Tigrinya's language. He couldn't get his tongue to form the hard consonants in almost every one of their words. In truth, he had a terrible ear for other languages.

It was then that part of the reason for Sam's incredible kindness was revealed.

"There has been a prophecy among my people, for as long as I can remember," Sam started. "My grandfather told a tale that spoke of an injured outsider who would one day fall upon our sands. This outsider would not be like us. Prophecy describes him as a pale man with skin as white as snow and hair the color of gold. It was said he would be lost and appear from nowhere, requiring help and guidance to find his way back to the light."

"And you think this pale man is me? That I'm some sort of prophet?" Paul said, almost choking on his coffee, casting the entire story as bunkum in his mind. "My hair isn't gold."

"Perhaps," Sam said. "Perhaps not. Only time will reveal those secrets."

"And what do we do in the meantime?"

"Today, we drink the coffee."

"And tomorrow?"

"Tomorrow, we work the fields," Sam said with a hearty laugh.

* * * * * *

The next morning, Sam woke Paul early.

It was still dark outside and Sam was dressed for work, wrapped and protected from the elements in loose all encompassing robes. He tossed Paul some clothes to match.

"Put these on, please."

"Where are we going?" Paul asked, suddenly nervous he had overstayed his welcome and was being shown to the curb.

"Now that you are feeling better, it is time for the next step in your recovery."

"Next step?"

Sam laughed, then whispered, "Yes. It is time, as you Americans say, to get back on your horse." Even at a whisper, his voice boomed.

Paul couldn't help but laugh. "But I don't have a horse," he snorted.

Sam smiled before pulling the wrap around his face. "Do not worry, my friend. I do."

Paul changed and joined Sam outside.

"Now this is how I like the desert," Paul said as he stared across the unmoving sand that rested beneath a purple sky.

"You will not feel that way once the sun rises, I assure you," Sam said.

"Probably not."

"Have you ever been a farmer, Paul?"

"I can't say that I have."

"Then not only will you get good exercise, but you will learn a new skill. Who knows, one day, this skill may come in handy."

Paul shrugged. "Anything's possible, I suppose."

"Perhaps you will also become a farmer."

"I wouldn't go that far."

Sam led Paul up the path to his crops on higher ground. It was largely barren ground, but miraculously, there were sprouts of green amongst the sand where Sam's labors had born fruit.

Together, the two of them worked the fields. It was arduous, backbreaking work, but surprisingly, Paul found himself enjoying it more than he could have expected. It was a good way to repay some of the kindness his new friend had shown him. Later, when on a short break to re-hydrate, Paul felt ready to collapse.

Sam, on the other hand, still stood tall.

"I've never seen an ox before today," Paul said. "Or smelled one either."

"My people have worked this land" —Sam spread his arms out to take in the entirety of the desert around them— "all of this land, for thousands of years. We have plowed the same soil, tilled the same dirt, moved the same rocks, and pushed back against the same sand. My family's history is right here."

He pointed at the crop.

"Everything that I am grows right there."

"I understand," Paul said.

"Is it not the same for you, my friend? Is there no place that holds your heart? No family history that binds you to a place?"

Paul sighed, deep in thought. Was there?

Sam said nothing.

"Metro City," Paul said.

"Me...ter...ro City," Sam said.

"Metro City."

"This is a real place?"

"Yes," Paul said.

"And this place is your home?"

"I was born there."

"That does not a home make," Sam said.

"Yeah. I know. Once upon a time, it was my home, I guess." Paul blew out a breath, felt his lip quiver a tick. "I never thought I'd see it again. When I left, there was never any consideration about going back. There was nothing there for me and, really, much of it was—is—a crime-ridden hovel. When I left I thought I was gone for good. I didn't think of it as home anymore."

Sanderson men don't show emotions. Paul stiffened as he once again heard his father's voice call out to him from the past. *Grow up, son.*

"And now you feel there is something in this Met...ro City for you?" Sam asked. "Something that was not there before?"

"Maybe," Paul said, shaking his head. He smiled at his own confusion. "I guess I miss it. I never thought I would, but I guess I do miss home."

"And your family?"

Paul's smile faded. "I have no family."

"That is where you are mistaken, my young friend," Sam said, clapping a firm hand on Paul's shoulder. "You are my brother and I am yours. I would not say it if it were not so."

"You're a good man, Sam. I'm lucky I found you."

"I found you," Sam said bluntly.

When Paul turned to look at him, Sam winked.

They both laughed.

* * * * * *

Sam didn't mention the prophecy again until some weeks later.

Paul had hoped that it had been a joke misunderstood in translation, but it hadn't been. After their nightly meal, Sam spoke to Paul in private. As the weeks had gone on, Sam's grasp of English, already decent, had improved even more. Paul was astonished at how easily he picked it up. He was like a living language sponge. He felt sure Sam could flourish with the tongue of any land were he there long enough.

Now seated, Sam reiterated the prophecy to Paul and told him in great detail about the pale visitor and the evils he would face in their stead.

"The prophecy of my people foretells that an outsider who has lost his way would come to us," Sam said, gently patting Paul's sunburned arm.

Paul winced at the touch. Every inch of him that had been exposed to the sun ached. Earlier that day, while working the field, he had taken off his wraps and went shirtless. Despite Sam's warning, Paul worked under the brutal desert sun and now he was paying the price for it. Mala had given him a salve that helped, but it could only do so much, especially in such short time. It was far less painful than the state he had been in when Sam found him in the desert, though.

"This outsider is described as a pale man, a white man who is easily burned by the sun. Does this seem at all familiar to you?"

Paul grimaced. "You put anybody with my skin tone out there and he's gonna burn, Sam."

"Perhaps. Perhaps not," Sam said. "The prophecy says when this white man arrives, he is to be guided into the rocky highlands, to the holy place near the peak of Emba Soira. There, a great final gift will be bestowed upon him and he in turn would become an even greater gift for mankind."

"You know how ridiculous this sounds right?"

"Perhaps. Perhaps not."

"Mmm, but you believe it anyway."

"I do."

"Why?"

"Faith."

"I'm going to need more than that."

"Faith is not something quantifiable, my young friend," Sam explained like a father telling his child the facts of life. "You either believe or you do not. I choose to believe. It is okay that you choose not to believe. Not believing does not make it not so."

"Just like believing doesn't automatically make it so."

Sam nodded. "Perhaps. Perhaps not."

"Am I the first sunburned white guy you've taken to this holy mountain retreat?"

Sam's features softened but he remained silent.

"You're not going to answer that, are you?" Paul probed.

Sam merely smiled in reply.

After a time, Paul spoke again. "I'm...I'm sorry, but I'm just a spoiled rich kid from Metro City. You've got the wrong guy. I'm no hero and I'm definitely nobody's savior."

"I do not believe this is so, my friend."

"One of us is going to be very disappointed, then," Paul joked.

"Perhaps," Sam said softly. "Perhaps not. Only time will tell."

"That's a lot of trust to place on me."

"You have strong shoulders," Sam said with a chuckle.

Paul wanted to retort, but stifled a yawn instead. After a long day working the fields, he was beyond tired.

"You should rest," Sam said as he doused the fire. "We have a big day tomorrow."

"Back to the field?"

"No," Sam said. His voice was deep and mysterious. "Tomorrow, we travel to the peak of Emba Soira. It's time you met the Holy One."

As Paul tried to drift off to sleep, he heard his father's voice loud and clear once more.

You're in deep now, my boy.

~ Chapter 9 ~

"Emba Soira?" Leena asked.

Paul turned to face her. "It's one of the highest peaks in Eritrea, rising nearly ten thousand feet high. It's a desolate mountain of dirt and rock, extremely difficult to reach and summit."

He continued with his tale.

* * * * * *

ERITREA – EIGHT YEARS EARLIER

The journey was long and difficult.

There was a reason excursions across the desert were generally taken by horse or in a vehicle of some kind. The desert heat was inhospitable and the sand blowing on the breeze made it feel like walking through sandpaper. Both Sam and Paul had to protect themselves for the long journey ahead of them.

Sam had packed extra water and provisions into two goatskin bags before he woke Paul that morning, Sam had reported. Each of them carried one of the hand-sewn packs on their backs, safely tucked beneath the traditional wrappings of the Tigrinya people. His identity was well hidden beneath the sweat-soaked head wrapping that made him look like a spiritual pilgrim on a journey to the Promised Land.

The last thing Paul felt was spiritual and he did not believe in ancient prophecies. The words of one of his heroes came back to him.

Hokey religions and ancient weapons are no match for a good blaster at your side, kid. There's no mystical energy field that controls my destiny.

To Paul, this prophecy his friend believed in was little more than superstitious mumbo jumbo. He had been raised to believe only in himself. His parents were not religious, except on Easter, Thanksgiving, and Christmas, the usual holidays where prayer was expected of them even in high society. The only time outside of holidays that Paul heard his father speak of God was while cursing, usually when some business deal of his went sour.

Whether it was real or not, Paul trusted Sam and, furthermore, he owed the man for saving his life. If taking a trip to see a holy man was important to Sam, then he would gladly accompany him, even if he did think it was arrant nonsense.

The sun was still hours from rising when they started on their trek across the desert. Sam wanted to get as far across the sands as they could before the sun came up and the temperature began its steady climb into triple digits.

Sam handed Paul a walking stick similar to the one he carried. It was old and well worn, the bark scrubbed smooth from years of abuse by the desert sands. It was a strong stick. Sam explained it would help him on their journey to Emba Soira.

Paul thought of the conversation they had before they left. "Are you ready to go?" Sam had asked as they finished their simple breakfast. Sam had opted not to wake Mala or the girls. They would slip out while the ladies slept.

"What if I say no?"

"We go anyway."

"Doesn't sound like much of a choice, does it?" Paul said.

"Prophecy is rarely about choice, my friend. It is about faith and destiny."

Paul looked down, suddenly very interested in the sand beneath them. "I thought about running," he admitted.

"You would run all the way to Emba Soira?" Sam asked.

Paul laughed. As usual, he was unsure if his friend was truly confused by the terminology or if he was just messing with him. Paul suspected the latter was more likely. Sam rarely passed up the opportunity to mess with him, especially now that his English was so good.

"I am your guide and your friend," Sam continued. "It is my job to get you to the holy temple atop Emba Soira. Everything else rests on your shoulders."

"Somebody is going to be disappointed," Paul said.

Sam shrugged. "We must all learn to deal with disappointments."

"And if I get up there to the top of this mountain..."

"Emba Soira."

"Right. What if I get up there and decide to throw myself off of it?"

"Then I will finally believe you are not the man we have been waiting for. Unless, of course, you survive the fall."

"Survive the..." Paul laughed. "You are a strange one, Sam."

"We should go."

Paul knew when he was beaten. He motioned toward the tent flap. "Lead the way, then."

"As you wish." Sam briefly bowed.

Snapped back to the present, Paul thought the first part of the trip felt like the daily walk to the fields where Sam's crops grew. Paul hoped they could survive without being tended to while he and Sam partook of what he considered a fool's errand. While walking, they chatted about abstract things. Sam wanted to know more about where Paul was from, so he regaled him with stories of Metro City. No matter how he framed it, the city never sounded that great, Paul thought. Heaven knew what Sam felt about it.

Once they passed the fields and the sun rose higher in the sky, the men traveled in silence to conserve energy. There was still a long journey ahead of them. Paul wished they could have brought the horses, but Sam said it was not permitted. Paul wanted to ask why not, but chose to save that question for another time.

As the day wore on, they kept going, only speaking when needed, namely concerning hazards in the sand or where the sand would give way to hard-packed dirt. Through it all, Paul could not shake the feeling he was being watched. It was impossible, of course. The only living soul as far as the eye could see was Sam. There was nobody else. Nobody.

He chalked it up to paranoia. He was still shaken by the massacre of his friends at the aid station. General Abdelkrim was still out there, somewhere. It was foolish to think he would still be after him, but who could understand the maniacal mind of a tyrant? Certainly not Paul.

Their destination, the mountain Emba Soira, sat off in the distance. It jutted out of the desert high into the clouds above.

It seemed so far away.

They spent the next several days walking along one perilous dirt track after another. They spoke infrequently, usually with Sam telling Paul more about the prophecy even though he really didn't want to hear it.

Paul's feet ached, then felt numb, but he kept pace with his guide. Sam had the stamina of a man half his age and showed no signs of fatigue or slowing down.

Emboldened by pride, Paul bit down on the pain and kept up.

Sanderson men don't quit, Paul, he heard his father's voice yell from a distant memory. Now was the time to prove it.

Days later, their food was beginning to run low as they reached the base of Emba Soira. Paul was limping by this point, but he kept going. The mountain was made of stone and earth, not an easy climb, but there were paths that marked where they could walk. Once they were to the first plateau, the path faded, leaving only intense rock climbing to continue their ascent.

From the desert floor, Paul could not see their destination at the peak, but now it was closer...yet still felt so far away.

"How much farther?" Paul asked.

"We are close. How is it you Americans say it—In the home stretch?"

Skeptical, Paul looked up at the peak, still hidden by clouds. "Uh huh. Should we look around for the easiest path?"

"There is only one true path to Emba Soira," Sam said.

"Let me guess," Paul said with a resigned sigh, "it's not the easy one."

"A hero's journey is never an easy one, my friend."

"I told you...I'm no hero."

"Perhaps. Perhaps not."

"I wish you'd stop saying that."

Paul felt sure Sam was smiling behind his head gear but there was no telling for sure. Sam pointed toward the path, such as it was. "Shall we continue?"

Paul let out a breath and motioned for him to take the lead. "After you."

The climb was not easy, but the two men made it to the rocky highlands before resting and enjoying a small respite with the last of the food they had brought with them. It was a fabulous meal that Mala had prepared for them before their journey.

Their next meal, if there was to be one, would be served at their destination, the holy temple of Emba Soira.

If they did not make it, they would surely starve to death, civilization in any direction too far away to help them.

There was still a long way to go so they got back underway as soon as their food had settled.

Paul felt a chill in the air and snow on the mountain above.

Like a Boy Scout, Sam was prepared. He had packed two goatskin coats they'd been using as bedrolls each night while they slept beneath the stars. On the mountain, they would also keep them warm.

"Boy, you don't miss a trick, do you?" Paul said.

Sam simply smiled.

"Exactly how many times have you made this trip?" Paul asked.

"A few."

"Mmm."

Paul didn't know what to think about that, but didn't press it. Sam was an intelligent man. He knew exactly what he was doing, exactly how to get to this fabled place atop Emba Soira. His thoughts drifted. Was it fate that brought him to Sam? Maybe. Paul wasn't a believer in fate or in much of anything, really, but even he noticed the coincidence of him making his way across the desert practically to Sam's door. There was a lot of desert out there to get lost in. Even a satellite would have had trouble finding him lost amongst all of that shifting sand. How was it Sam found him? Luck? Or was that what fate really was—just plain, simple, dumb luck? Paul had no idea.

These questions and more rattled around in Paul's brain during the journey.

Once they reached the peak, the holy man of the mountain—if he even existed—would tell Sam Paul was not the heroic stranger they expected and they could be on their way.

It took the better part of a day to reach the summit.

Sam and Paul rested on the flat, rocky outcropping, each man winded, tired, and very hungry. If there were any signs of life atop Emba Soira, they were hidden by the thick canopy of fog, bitter winds, and thick, wet snow. The wind grew in intensity the higher they climbed, slicing through their clothes like ice. Not even their heavy winter coats kept out the cold for long.

As Paul predicted, there were no shortcuts up the mountain. The way to the peak was a dizzying route that went every direction except the most direct. It reminded him of one of those old *The Family Circus* comic strips he used to read when he was a kid. Sam must have learned his sense of direction from those kids. As if.

"Is this it?" Paul asked as he pulled himself over a rock onto the closest thing he had seen to flat ground since their last rest stop. He couldn't see anything that resembled a shack, much less a holy place. The only thing waiting for him there was snow and ice and a bitterly cold wind.

"Yes. We are almost there."

"I don't see it! Where is this holy place of yours?"

Sam pointed to a spot somewhere above. Just a short climb remained, but all Paul saw was fog.

"I can't see anything!" Paul shouted over the high-pitched howling of the wind.

Then, as if by some miracle, the wind suddenly stopped and the fog parted.

Silence descended on Emba Soira.

"It is there," Sam said, pointing. "Do you see?"

It was as if the clouds had parted and God now rained sunshine down upon them. Paul squinted and could just make out a small dwelling made of stone and timber at the top of a rocky outcrop a small distance ahead. There was nothing fancy at all about the building, but with its dark red painted walls, it looked as out of place among the inhospitable terrain as Paul felt. It was the size of a small house, two stories tall. The design was simple and unassuming. A basic set of stairs led the rest of the way up to the temple's front door.

"I see it," Paul whispered. "How is this possible?"

"Faith," was all Sam said before moving on.

Paul shook his head and followed.

It was a short climb compared to the one they had taken to get that far. By this time, Paul was in excruciating pain, but his curiosity now had the better of him. He wanted to see what was inside this so-called monastery. He hoped it was worth the time and pain it had taken to reach it.

Paul's heart wildly beat in his chest. He had no idea what he would find inside the strange dwelling, but for the first time since he and Sam had started their journey, he had this feeling deep within it was indeed his destiny to be there. Perhaps it was fate after all.

Not that he planned to admit that to Sam.

As they approached the front entrance, Paul noticed the building was older than he had previously thought. The walls were weathered by years of abuse in such a fierce climate. Still, for its age, it was well kept and maintained. The paint appeared fresh, maybe only a year old. Someone had to live there. He only hoped they were home. And welcoming.

"It would be a shame to come all this way and nobody's home," he told Sam.

"The holy man is there," Sam said with certainty.

Pushing open the unlocked, heavy wooden door, Paul and Sam found an open-plan room filled with various ancient stone tablets as well as many pillows littering the floor like one of the dorm rooms at a local college. Seated on one of the pillows at the farthest end of the room directly in front of them was an old man who looked, on first glance, to be around one hundred years old.

He was alone.

The old man was thin and lanky, with a long white beard and bushy eyebrows. His head was clean-shaven. The beard started at his ears and was well manicured. He sat cross-legged on the pillow, his eyes shut, his breathing slow and measured. He looked at peace.

To their right, a large open fireplace blazed, fighting back the cold air from the open door.

Sam eased the well-oiled door shut until the lock caught with an audible *SNAP!*

The holy man's eyes flew open.

"So," the holy man said softly, "you have come at last, my child."

Paul took a cautious step forward. "Are you...are you talking to me?"

"Of course," the old man said. "I have been expecting you."

Paul turned to Sam. "Did you tell him we were coming?"

Sam shook his head.

"Come, sit before me, Mr. Sanderson," the old man said. His voice was even, measured, with only the barest hint of the cracking brought on by age.

He knows my name.

He nodded as he took a seat on the offered pillow directly in front of the old man.

Sam chose not to sit. Instead, he took up position standing behind his young friend. Paul felt protected knowing Sam had his back.

"How did...how do you know my name?" Paul asked.

"I know many things," the holy man replied with only the barest hint of amusement. "Including your language."

"I...I don't know what to say. I don't know about any of this."

"I know a lot about you, including the great need for knowledge you carry inside. Your search for a meaning to your life has taken you on a journey of danger and discovery.

You have traveled the world in search of something you cannot fully explain. That journey ultimately brought you to this place. Now that you have arrived, we will work to fill the great emptiness you feel deep inside. In time, perhaps we can answer all of your questions." The old man's voice was like audible honey: soft and creamy.

"How could you..." Paul started and got to his feet. "I've never told anyone that. Not even Sam..."

The old man stood as well. He was short, but surprisingly nimble for a man of his apparent advanced years. "Come, my friends," the old man offered. He motioned toward the roaring fire. "Warm yourselves beside the fire while I prepare a meal in your honor. You must be famished after your long journey. We shall continue our talk after we dine. There is a great deal I need to teach you, Mr. Sanderson. It will not be easy, but there is only a limited time for you to learn the secrets of Emba Soira."

"Why limited?"

The holy man smiled. "Perhaps he is blind," the old man said to Sam. "Can he not see that I am an old man?"

Paul stared at the old man, unsure what to say. He was afraid he had offended him and wasn't sure if he should apologize or remain silent. Silence won out.

"Why are you here, Mr. Sanderson?" the old man asked.

"I...I don't really know."

He smiled. "That is a good beginning."

"Really?"

"Yes. It is difficult to teach a man who believes he knows the answers."

Paul scratched the side of his head. "That makes sense, I guess."

"The question then becomes, are you ready to discover the truth about yourself, Paul Sanderson? Are you ready to learn the secrets of this sacred place?"

"Yes," Paul said, answering on reflex.

"Are you certain?"

Suddenly, Paul's heart began to race, but there was no backing out now. "Yes."

"Good."

* * * * * *

Paul Sanderson stood on the rocks and looked out at the sea of sand far below.

The desert heat seemed so far away from him after a day in the winter wonderland at the top of the mountain. He could still see the desert from his new perch and he could still feel the pain and itch from his blistered skin, but even that pain was beginning to fade thanks to the salve the old man had given him the night before.

Sleeping in an actual bed was a nice bonus. It had been too long since he had slept on a mattress or used a pillow. Compared to the accommodations at the aid station and Sam's family tent, his borrowed room at the monastery was like staying in a five star hotel.

He watched the sunrise surrounded by the snows on top of Emba Soira. From that height, everything else he knew seemed so far away, but the feeling he was being watched remained and he couldn't explain why. The three of them were very much alone on top of the mountain.

"Are you planning to jump?"

Paul smiled, but did not turn to see who was walking up behind him. He recognized the accented voice. Plus, he had heard his boots crunch in the ice-topped snow.

"Thinking about it," Paul said in a manner that told his friend he was joking.

"Long way down," Sam said matter-of-fact.

"Who knows, maybe I'd survive? Oh, wouldn't it be cool if I could fly?"

"I assume this is more of your American humor."

"Perhaps. Perhaps not."

They stood there in silence, smiling at each other, only the icy wind blowing between them.

"You've come to tell me you're leaving, aren't you?" Paul said a few moments later.

"Yes. It is time," Sam said.

"Don't want to stick around and watch me fail miserably at this, huh?"

"On the contrary. I expect you to thrive."

"That makes one of us at least."

"Know that if the worst happens and you are not the chosen one spoken of in the prophecy, you will always be welcome in my home."

"That's very kind of you, Sam."

"It is the way of my people. Of my family. Prophecy or no, you are my brother, now and forever."

"Give my love to Mala and the girls," Paul said. "Tell them thank you from me and I hope to see them again."

"I will tell them. When I found you alone in the sand, you were a stranger to me. Now, you have become a part of my family, Paul Sanderson, you and your silly American name." He laughed. "From now until the end of time and beyond, we are family."

"Thanks, Sam. I'll miss you."

The two men shook hands and Paul pulled Sam into a bear hug.

"I'm going to miss you," he repeated. "I can never repay you for your kindness."

"There is no need," Sam said. "And now, I must make my way home. It is a long journey back."

With a final wave, Sam started down the rough-hewn path to the desert below where his family—his life—waited for him.

Paul envied him. His friend had found the one thing that Paul had been searching for all of his life: family, home, peace and contentment. Paul had spent half of his life desiring those things, begging for them even. The rest of his life he had spent running as far away from them as possible.

Standing on a mountain in subzero winds, Paul Sanderson missed his home. He had tried to fight it, but the truth was he yearned to see Metro City and all of its dirty corners and impersonal steel and concrete buildings once more. Most of all, he really missed central heating and air. If nothing else, his visit to Africa had made him miss the convenient comforts of city life. He even looked forward to reconnecting with the people of Metro City, although some more than others.

He also realized that he missed his parents. Despite all the heartache, he missed them. He missed his home.

At the moment, however, Metro City seemed so very far away.

"Are you ready, my son?" an aged voice creaked.

Startled, Paul spun to face the holy man of Emba Soira. He hadn't heard the old man approach like he had Sam. Apparently, stealth *was* possible in snow and ice. He was either a ninja or the old man could fly. At that moment, he wasn't willing to rule out either theory.

"Ready for what?" he said.

The old man smiled. "To begin."

~ Chapter 10 ~

The passing of time was a mysterious thing there.

The days and weeks had long since begun to blur together, as they had when he'd been staying with Sam. The ebb and flow of time had become immaterial until he could no longer discern one day from the next. When the holy man had said they were ready to begin, Paul hadn't known what to expect. Nowhere in his mind's eye would he have ever predicted how his days would play out. Each day started the same as the one before it and ended with him aching and exhausted—day in day out. The old man, and that was all Paul knew to call him —that or Master, which also felt somewhat out of place—made them a simple meal each morning. And each morning, they ate in silence, meditating on the day's journey ahead of them. Or in Paul's case, dreading it.

While his new friend prepared the meal, Paul made a trek partway down the mountain to a fresh spring where he collected two containers full of clean water for their daily use. Paul tied each container to a long stick that he supported on his shoulders. Of course, nothing was that simple where the old man was concerned. The path to and from the spring was an obstacle course he had to overcome. If he fell or spilled the water, even a drop, he would then have to go back down the mountain, refill the containers, and start the obstacle course all over again. In those first days, Paul had made many repeat trips, but eventually his balance improved and he was able to endure the course without incident.

Paul cheered this accomplishment.

The old man simply nodded.

The next morning, he was shocked to find the obstacle course had been altered to present a more difficult challenge.

How dare he do this to me? Who does he think he is?

But then he realized it was just an added aspect to his training and he would have to learn any problem could have more than one solution. He had to be able to change tactics no matter what the world threw at him.

Like everything else atop Emba Soira, this was a test, one he was determined to pass.

Paul let out a hearty laugh as he started down the mountain to fetch the day's water.

A few steps down and he turned to spy the old man watching from a small window, a smile over his face.

Meditating was Paul's least favorite activity, as it was the one thing he found himself to be truly lousy at, but he tried to follow the example the old man laid out for him. Most of the time, he simply fell asleep until the old man's disappointed grunt woke him from a restful slumber.

Then they would train for several hours after breakfast, learning new ways to fight, to climb, to run, to carry, to break down and to rebuild. Paul moved timber from one end of the courtyard to the other, sometimes carrying the heavy wooden posts up the snow-covered rise to the rocks above where the old man was building a new garden to grow vegetables. The journey was hard and the labor taxing, but after a few days, the timber felt lighter, easier to carry.

Stretching was also an important part of the day. Paul stretched before and after each training session to keep his muscles from cramping up. The old man's techniques were unusual, but they worked. Paul was more limber than he had ever been. He felt lighter on his feet. Stronger.

Then, they returned to the courtyard where more timber waited to be moved. Paul began to suspect the old man had helpers hidden away to create work for him to do while meditating.

Then came more training.

The old man was a tough old bird. Paul had taken some martial arts classes while in college and thought he was pretty good at it until his first lesson on Emba Soira. The old man was fast and he never missed his mark. It would take time, but Paul eventually began to pick up the disciplines his new teacher offered. With enough time and practice, he might one day be able to beat the old man in a sparring session.

After several hours of intense training, they enjoyed another small meal in silence. The old man prepared the meal and they ate sitting on pillows on the floor, near the fire. Since the holy man made lunch, Paul took care of the cleanup afterwards. He actually found washing dishes quite calming. After lunch, more meditation followed, which led to more napping and another disapproving grunt.

Afterwards, Paul found himself immersed in intense study.

The old man's library was a thing of beauty, probably the one room in the place where Paul felt most at home. Unlike the other rooms, with their simple and even crude design aesthetic, the library walls were made of wood, deeply stained and polished until they shined. It was also the only carpeted room he had seen since he arrived in Africa, the carpet a deep burgundy and soft on his bare feet.

It felt like the library at home in Sanderson House.

The bookshelves were intricately designed and held hundreds—if not thousands—of tomes as well as clay pots filled with rolled scrolls printed on papyrus leaf. There was a sense of history in the room, not just from all the knowledge contained in the writings, but with the thought of the old man, and perhaps generations of men before him, learning and growing within it.

The library back home was his father's favorite room, and it had been one of Paul's favorite places growing up as well. As a child he had been a voracious reader. It didn't matter the subject. He enjoyed non-fiction as much as fiction, but adventure stories were his favorites. Paul loved the old pulp characters, each one larger than life as they traveled the world fighting would-be world conquerors and monsters too incredible to be real. In the end, a love of reading was probably the only thing he and his father had in common. Perhaps that was why he loved the Sanderson library so much —it was the one room where he felt a certain closeness with his father.

The monastery's library was filled with eclectic editions containing ancient secrets, religious teachings, the storied histories of not only the Bihére-Tigrinya—Sam's people—but of all of the Tigrinya tribes. They had a rich history and a shared common cultural background, but also one filled with death and despair. The Bihére-Tigrinya inhabited central Eritrea, their people making up somewhere around fifty-five percent of the population. In more recent times their numbers had swelled to above three million. The land they called home spanned the southern and central regions of the country, as well as the Northern Red Sea and Anseba areas, but they still resided mostly in the Eritrean highlands. The Tigrinyas or Eritra were related to the Tigrayans of Ethiopia and both spoke Tigrinya, an ancient Ethiopian Semitic language belonging to the Afro-Asiatic family. The old man told Paul they were devout followers of the Eritrean Orthodox Tewahedo Church. Then there was the coming of the warlords and the rise to power of General Abdelkrim. Not much was known of the general's background, but what *was* known was contained in the old man's notebooks. Abdelkrim was a self-appointed general. He had not risen through the ranks nor attained his position through hard work. He stole his position through treachery and cruelty and, with an army at his beck and call, took control over Eritrea and her people. He was not even a local, having appeared in the country from an unknown land some years back. Nothing more was known of the Cobra's history.

Paul read with interest. The general's brutality haunted his dreams at night. He didn't know how and didn't know when, but one day, General Abdelkrim would get what was coming to him. Justice would finally be served. Paul hoped he was there to see it when it happened.

Over time, the old man introduced Paul to the histories of other lands, other peoples, all over the world. As he soaked up all the knowledge being offered to him, he realized he knew little of the history of his own country or, indeed, his own city. There was so much he did not know about his homeland or his family and how instrumental they were to Metro's growing pains and survival. He vowed there and then to learn as much as possible as soon as he was able.

Another scroll shared the secrets of Emba Soira and explained why the old man's order had chosen it as their base of operations. Paul found it a fascinating read involving ancient sects, hidden worlds, and monsters beyond imagining. The scroll also prophesied that a savior would rise from the depths of Hell's embrace to save them all.

More mythology, Paul mused. *This can't be about me.*

The next scroll talked about something called the Eyes of Judgment. Oddly enough, whomever wrote the scrolls pertaining to whatever this Judgment Stare was kept the details of it vague. This was unusual, particularly when compared to the in-depth information contained within all the other texts and scrolls he had thus far perused.

When Paul asked about the Eyes of Judgment, the old man simply shook his head and said, "It is not yet time, my son. Patience."

Paul was never much of a patient man and what little he had he was quickly running out of, especially when he felt the old man was holding back on him.

The library had information spanning centuries, and Paul devoured everything he could. He even had a good laugh when he found a small stash of old pulp novels hidden away on one of the older bookcases. He wondered whom they had belonged to because they did not seem to be his teacher's taste in reading material and were certainly out of place in a location such as this.

Each day, they would study a new text, and Paul also shared stories about Metro City with his new mentor. The old man carefully inscribed the stories into a notebook, preserving them for posterity's sake. He felt all knowledge had to be recorded so that future generations could learn from them no matter what the subject.

Paul enjoyed listening to the old man tell stories. His voice, deep in timbre, reminded him of Sam and his boisterous laughter while spinning yarns for his daughters. The old man shared a similar rich baritone, though his was somewhat cracked with age. Paul wondered how old his master truly was, but he was far too smart to ask. Or too scared.

Between the training and the chores, there wasn't a muscle in Paul's body that didn't ache. He had done more manual labor since he had arrived at the monastery than in all of his years to that point combined. He was leaner than he had ever been and his muscles were stronger as well, but still Paul did not feel he was any closer to being this prophesied savior he was supposed to be since he had heard Sam first mention it. He still thought the whole thing a load of bunkum. Yet, he couldn't explain the old man, and how he knew so much about him, about this place and the magic he felt there. It was all still such a mystery.

After a small but hearty dinner, they set about their daily evening chores. Since they were the only ones currently residing in the temple, or so Paul was led to believe—and he had seen no one but the old man since he arrived there—it fell to them to keep it clean and tidy. The old man swept while Paul mopped and washed their dishes. Together, they wiped down the walls and shelves, keeping away what little dust accumulated.

Still, he did it all without complaint, becoming used to the daily grind and routine.

After cleaning, they went on a short hike across the mountainside followed by more meditation, which was then followed by sleep, blessed sleep. The old man trained Paul in both body and mind, teaching him the wisdom of his ancient race. Such studies were taxing, so Paul easily slept through the night, thanks in no small part to pure exhaustion. His dreams were anything but restful, however. When he wasn't dreaming about his father or mother, which had become an all too common occurrence since he heard of their passing, he was reliving the massacre at the aid station.

In these dreams, everything moved around him in slow motion.

He helplessly watched as the first of General Abdelkrim's men arrived at the camp. Like his namesake, the Cobra, the general was dangerous, stealthy, deadly, and quick to strike. In the dream, Abdelkrim's scar appeared to move, hissing at him as though alive.

It was always the same. Paul was forced to watch his friends and colleagues die over and over again. Sometimes the dream would change and they died in different ways than what happened in reality. Those nightmares were the hardest.

The only constant in the dreams was Paul's inability to save his friends.

Jay Perry, Pamela Requard, Samantha Winters, Marcus Rawston, Wayne Ash, Tyler Hawkins, Judy Hess, and most of the native villagers in the camp to help out or to receive aid were cut down in front of him. Even though Paul had not actually seen all of them die, in his dreams he saw their grisly fate. In his dreams, *everyone* perished.

Everyone but him.

He still did not understand why.

Fortune favors the bold, Paul heard his father tell him.

"But I wasn't bold," Paul muttered.

Then he woke up.

It was dark outside.

There was no clock to tell him the time, but it really didn't matter. Time seemed immaterial atop Emba Soira. He no longer had his father's watch, having lost it somewhere along the way. He hoped that he had left it at Sam's hut. The thought of it being lost, sandblasted away to nothingness in the desert, filled him with a sense of dread...and sadness. For all the years he had spent not caring for anything belonging to the man, that watch now represented all he had left of the father he'd barely known. He had come to regret his part in the divide that existed between father and son: two stubborn men who were more alike than either cared to admit.

I should have called him, should have tried to bridge the gap somehow, Paul thought, but it was too late now.

It was far too late.

Paul sat up on the edge of the cot and stretched the kinks out of his tired, sore body. He slipped his cold feet into a pair of socks then into the slippers the old man had left for him after his first week there. He had also been gifted with fresh clothes to wear while training. The slippers were warm and surprisingly comfortable for being handmade out of furry animal hide. Like Sam, the old man of the mountain knew how to survive with what the land had to offer, which wasn't much as far as Paul could ascertain.

As inhospitable as the desert had been, and it was brutal, Paul believed living atop Emba Soira was even more so. The desert had tried to kill him and failed. Paul was certain that when—not if—the mountain decided to kill him, there would be no hope of escape.

With his blanket wrapped around him, Paul headed for the main room to stoke the fire and maybe find a small snack to tide him over until breakfast, which was still a few hours away.

I'd kill for a candy bar, he thought. His stomach growled at the thought.

He knew there would be no candy bars hidden in the kitchen and almost certainly no junk food of any kind. Such was not the ways of the old man.

In some ways, Paul was not surprised to find the old man already awake and preparing their breakfast. He started to ask how he had known he would wake early, but decided not to bother because there would be no straight answer. His friend loved to speak in riddles.

"Good morning," the old man said in his stilted English. He was never at a loss for words, but his delivery sometimes reminded Paul of a character out of an old movie.

"Good morning," Paul replied. "What time is it?"

The old man looked left then right before answering. "Morning," he said.

"So glad we cleared that up," Paul muttered as he crouched in front of the fire. The warmth felt good and sensation began to return to his toes.

"I beg your pardon?" the old man said.

"Don't you ever sleep?" Paul asked, changing the subject.

"Yes, though my people apparently do not require as much rest as you Americans."

"Did you just make a joke?" Paul asked, astonished. In all of the time he had been there, he could not recall his aged mentor ever attempt at being humorous. At least not intentionally.

Maybe I'm rubbing off on him, Paul thought.

"I am a very funny man," the old man said. "Ask anyone."

"Well, you are the funniest man on this mountain," Paul said.

"Yes, I am."

Paul smiled. "Walked right into that one."

"Yes, you did."

The old man handed Paul a small bowl filled with vegetables and lightly cooked fish. There were no forks in the kitchen, just spoons for soup and chopsticks for everything else but, thankfully, Paul had mastered their use while in college so he never had to resort to eating with his fingers. He still wasn't sure where the old man found fresh fish each day. It wasn't like there was a lake on top of the frozen tundra outside their door, and the fresh well-fed spring he visited each morning did not have fish. Not that he would put it past the old man to climb down the mountain to a lower plateau in the dark, find a lake somewhere just below the snowline, and be back before dawn with fresh fish for breakfast. Nope, that would not surprise him at all.

As usual, they ate in silence until the old man said, "Are you satisfied with your training?"

"Satisfied?" Paul must have looked confused.

"Do you think you have learned all that you can here?" the old man added.

"No, sir. We can never learn all that we can."

"Correct. We are always learning new things, my son."

Here we go, Paul thought. *Another test. I knew it.*

"I seem to recall you saying something like that not too long ago," Paul said.

"That must have been the day you were paying attention," the old man said.

Paul stared at him.

The old man cracked a grin.

"You *are* a funny man this morning," Paul said.

"Yes." He plopped a morsel of fish into his mouth to hide the smile. "I am in a...how you say...good mood this morning."

"That's good," Paul said. "I'm glad one of us got some sleep."

"I sleep like a baby," the old man said.

"Why are you asking me about this now?" Paul queried, getting back on topic. "Are you trying to get rid of me or something?"

"Not at all," the old man said softly. "You are part of this place now. Its doors will always be open to you, but we both know you will not remain on this mountain forever."

Paul started to speak, but the old man cut him off.

"No. There is another place that has a hold on your heart, Paul Sanderson. To deny it is useless. I knew it the moment I met you and I believe you know it as well. One day you will return to your home."

"I have no home," Paul said.

It was something he said anytime someone asked him where he was from or about where he grew up, so much so the answer had become second nature to him. It was a convenient lie, one that protected him from the harsh memories he wanted to keep buried. At some point along the way, the lie stopped being for those who asked and became as much a lie to Paul himself.

"Your true home calls out to you," the old man said. "The only question is whether or not you will answer her summons."

Paul remained silent and thought before answering. Perhaps it was time to stop lying to everyone and, especially, to himself. The old man knew him so well. "I guess it's time I stopped lying to myself."

"You guess?"

Paul pursed his lips. "I know."

"I agree."

"Are you asking me to leave?"

The old man chuckled. He motioned toward the large open room. "No. As I said, you are welcome to stay in this place as long as you like. Plus, I enjoy the company."

"Then I will stay...just a little bit longer," Paul said.

"Then I think you are ready."

"Ready?" Paul said, confused. "Ready for what? You've been hinting at something more for some time, but—"

The old man smiled. "It has been a good morning," he said as if that explained everything. It didn't, at least not to Paul.

Up to that point, the old man had been a stern, albeit kind, teacher, a tough headmaster and often just a grumpy old man. This playful side of him was a welcome change and Paul hoped to see more of this from his mentor.

"But what do you think, my son. Do you think you are ready?"

Paul set down his breakfast and took in a deep, cleansing breath, then let it out. He didn't know what to expect, but he knew it was time to move forward, time to take the next step.

"Yes," he said. "Yes, I am."

~ Chapter 11 ~

The old man led Paul to a room he had not visited before.

The hallway leading to it was hidden behind a panel in the wall in a far corner of the main room. Paul watched with amazement as the panel slid aside on a wheeled track in the wall when the old man pushed his hand against a specific spot on it. The old man led the way down the narrow hall until they came to a black door. Inset into the inky blackness was a set of what looked like eyes belonging to an angry demon.

"What is this place?" Paul asked, equally curious and terrified of the answer.

"The chamber of the Eyes of Judgment."

"Sounds ominous."

"Yes." Apparently, the time for levity was behind them. The old man motioned toward the door. "You must enter this room of your own volition, Paul Sanderson. It must be your decision alone that brings you to this place."

"So I can just turn around and go get some more breakfast if I want?"

"If that is your desire, yes," the old man said. "I hope, however, that you are intelligent enough to understand the gift that awaits you on the other side of that door. This gift is not bestowed lightly. It is your destiny."

"Oh no," Paul started. "Not that...prophecy again."

"Yes," the old man said. "Now it must be fulfilled. It is time. You are ready. But I must warn you...there are dangers."

"No offense," Paul said. He was growing tired of the riddles and double talk. "But I've almost died fifty times since I got here, not to mention all the crap I went through just to get here. This whole country is dangerous. Why should this door be any different?"

"As you wish," the old man said with a nod. "I can say no more."

He opened the door. Unlike the rest of the doors in the place, this one creaked on rusty hinges. That confirmed Paul's suspicions this room was not visited often, if at all.

Compared to the rest of the place he now called home, the room was Spartan. Curtains of a deep rustic red that matched the outside walls hung from the ceiling all around them, obscuring the dark painted walls. There were no windows. The room was dark; the only light in the room emanated from a circle of six candles of various sizes and shapes burning in the center of it. A fine haze hovered near the ceiling that was painted black. Paul wondered how and when the candles and fire had been lit. Mystery upon mystery.

Unlike the other rooms, there were not even pillows on the floor for them to sit upon.

In the center of the circle of candles sat a ceramic bowl filled with a bubbling golden-hued liquid. Steam rose from the plate, adding to the haze above.

I'm sorry, son, he heard his father's voice say. He sounded so far away now.

The old man sat cross-legged on the hardwood floor in front of the candles and motioned for Paul to do likewise and sit across from him.

Paul was nervous but he had learned to trust the old man during his time here as his guest. There was no reason to suspect he would try to harm him now. He sat slowly, wishing he had a pillow.

"My son," the old man said, his voice softer than Paul had ever heard it. "During your brief stay here, it has been my honor to impart to you wisdom, patience, and physical strength based on the teachings of my people. Though you have been at times a challenging pupil, you have ultimately excelled at every task I placed before you. I believe you are finally ready to receive the final gift this humble place can bestow upon you. It is your destiny."

"Sam kept telling me this story over and over again, about this and that. About me being some sort of savior. I told him then and now I have to tell—"

"You have been seeking a purpose your entire life," the old man said. "Your desire to help people is what ultimately brought you here...to this place...to me...and now to this sacred room. It is also that purpose that will ultimately take you away from this place."

No, Paul thought, but wisely chose not to say so aloud. *What brought me here was my* inability *to help others. I couldn't save them. I couldn't save Judy. I couldn't save...my parents.*

"It has been an honor to train with you, Master," Paul said. It was the first time he had called him by such a title, but the timing seemed appropriate.

The old man nodded.

Paul returned the gesture.

The old man lifted the small bowl from the circle of candles. He whispered a prayer in a language Paul could scarcely comprehend over the steaming liquid then handed it across to his student.

"Drink this, my son. It is a mixture of herbs and minerals mostly unknown to western science. A recipe lost to all but me. As you drink, I will recite the words passed down from an ancient text and you will be reborn."

Reborn? Paul thought. He wasn't sure he liked how that sounded, but a moment passed, and then, holding the bowl aloft, he felt a strange sense of serenity, of contentment. All doubts disappeared...and he was ready.

He lifted the bowl to his lips. His first sip was tentative, cautious, but the liquid did not scald his tongue so he turned the bowl up and drank deeply of the mysterious elixir. It was bitter, like a musty tea, but thicker than flavored water. It was not the worst thing he had sampled since climbing to the top of the mountain.

The old man began to speak.

Paul could not understand the language his master spoke, but as he recited the ancient incantation, the room started to spin around them. He felt dizzy, his eyes going in and out of focus as though he had been staring at something for far too long. He swore the curtains covering the walls began to move even though he was positive he was not moving around the room, but still very much rooted to the spot where he had sat down. Sweat began to bead his brow.

Where's that heat coming from?

It did not take long to receive an answer.

From deep within his gut, Paul Sanderson began to burn.

Wrenched in incredible agony, he dropped the bowl and it shattered into tiny shards. The pain was incredible, beyond anything he had ever felt before. Even nearly dying in the desert had not burned as harshly as this. It was as though his insides were being hollowed out and replaced with the flames of Hell.

It was almost more than he could bear.

Almost.

Through sheer force of will, through the skills of meditation he had finally mastered, he held tight against the pain.

Paul lurched, then fell over, his face slamming into the hardwood floor.

As he writhed in agony, a sickly yellow vapor seeped from Paul's eyes, nose and mouth as though he were possessed by some ethereal spirit.

He felt like he was dying.

He wanted to die.

Sanderson men don't quit, his father's voice yelled.

"I don't care!" Paul shouted.

The old man continued speaking the unknown language, faster now as the room spun quicker and quicker.

"What...what's happening to me?" Paul managed to get out as he somehow pushed himself back into a seated position. "My insides feel like they're on fire! Why...why are you doing this...to me?"

The old man's voice grew louder.

The candles erupted into a geyser of flame around them.

Paul pulled at his clothes. They were suddenly too tight...constricting.

Fabric tore and fell away.

"What have you done to me?" Paul shouted.

The old man's voice grew louder but he did not answer.

Paul ripped at his clothes, the rest of his shirt falling away in tatters.

From his chest, flames leapt outward.

Paul screamed, his voice a mixture of pain and fear.

He looked down and saw two eye-shaped images burning brightly on his chest.

What the hell is that?

The eyes were ablaze.

His chest was on fire.

Paul screamed again.

The old man's voice grew louder as a bitter, icy wind blew through the room, dancing in concert with the smoke and the flames, a dizzying concerto that made Paul want to throw up even more. The room spun around him as though caught in the grip of a force five hurricane.

The old man's voice suddenly fell silent.

The room spun faster and faster until—

The fire consumed him.

Paul Sanderson screamed. His flesh burned, growing hotter and hotter with each passing second.

He wasn't sure how much more pain he could withstand.

And then, as suddenly as it began, peace descended upon the room.

The eyes on his chest were gone.

The pain, the excruciating pain, was also gone.

In the dim light of a lone candle, Paul Sanderson threw up.

The old man stared across the void at him in silence, not smiling, but also not scowling. Then the last candle flickered out and plunged everything into darkness.

Seconds ticked off in silence.

Then Paul coughed—

—and vomited again.

One candle ignited on its own, the renewed flame chasing the shadows to the far corners of the room.

Paul Sanderson slowly got to his feet, still nauseated and off balance. The experience had changed him, that much was certain. There was something different about him now. He couldn't explain it, but he felt it to be true. He flexed his muscles and, surprisingly, they no longer hurt as severely as they had before. The searing pain within him was gone and there was no sign he had been burned by the flames that had engulfed his torso.

Paul felt stronger than he ever had before, re-energized and rejuvenated. Most importantly, he felt whole. The gnawing chasm within his very soul was no more.

He *was* reborn.

That word suddenly meant something to him.

Sanderson men have to be strong, his father said.

Paul took in the room. It was as though the chaos of the last few moments had been erased...or had it all been a dream? A drug-induced hallucination? He couldn't say for sure. All he knew was that something magnificent had happened to him, something he could not adequately put into words.

The old man remained seated across from him. He looked up at Paul in silence, perhaps appearing hopeful that all had gone well.

Paul wiped the vomit and spittle from his lips and chin then lowered himself back to the floor, kneeling instead of sitting. He looked across the candles to the old man for guidance. "What happened? I don't understand any of this."

The old man smiled at his pupil. "My son, you have been given that which you have been searching for these long years: True meaning to your life. Now you also have the power to take that to a higher level, to help people on an even greater scale. Was that not what you wished for?"

"Yes, I..." Paul started, confused by all that had transpired. "Yes."

"You have been endowed with the Eyes of Judgment, Paul Sanderson of Metro City," the old man said as though it was the most common thing anyone could say.

"The Eyes of...what?" Paul stammered in utter confusion.

The old man stood and bade his student to follow. Paul fell into step beside him.

"The Eyes of Judgment," the old man repeated as they walked. "It is a mystical energy that now resides within you. All evildoers who are forced to gaze into their fire—the Judgment Stare—will burn with the pain and guilt of all their victims combined until justice has been served."

"You're...are you serious?" Paul said. It all sounded so far-fetched even after all he'd just experienced.

"I am."

"How does it work?"

"I will train you in its use, my son. You need not fear. You have been chosen. The prophecy has been fulfilled."

"I...I don't know what to say," Paul said as confused as ever.

The old man placed a reassuring hand on Paul's shoulder as they returned to the communal area where they first met. "Come. Let us find you a new shirt." The old man walked beside him down another hallway. "As has been prophesied, you will use the Eyes of Judgment to purge those who would do evil of their sins. You will be the one to show them the path of righteousness and then lead them down that path."

"Sounds like you want me to be a preacher," Paul said. "I'm not...I've never been big on religion."

"It is not about religion, my son. It is about justice. You will bring justice to the unjust. I will train you how to effectively use the Eyes of Judgment. You will learn what you are capable of accomplishing and how best to use this new power for good."

Paul was dumbstruck.

The old man grabbed him by the arms in a fatherly fashion and smiled. "Your journey of enlightenment is almost at an end, but a new journey, a far more dangerous one, awaits you outside these walls. Come...there is still much to learn."

Before Paul could say anything more, the front door exploded open.

~ Chapter 12 ~

Wood splintered as the heavy door exploded inward.

Paul and the old man were caught unawares and knocked off their feet by the deafening concussive force of the detonation. Paul slammed into the hearth, felt the warm bricks against his back. The old man slid across the freshly polished floor Paul had cleaned by hand the night before. He came to rest by the wall.

Smoke and flame filled every nook and cranny, climbing up the walls like a giant caterpillar. Hungry, the fire spread quickly.

Shaken but otherwise uninjured by the blast, Paul pushed himself off the floor. His head spun and his ears rang. It was hard to see through the haze and smoke, but he knew they wouldn't be alone for very long. "What hit us?" he croaked, choking on the thick smoke.

The old man coughed and pushed himself up into a crouch. It was the first time Paul had seen his friend look unsteady.

"We're about to have company!" Paul shouted.

"I know," the old man said softly, coughing again. "I had hoped there would be more time."

"More time?" Paul asked.

A cold snap hit them as the wintry winds of Emba Soira flooded into the hall. The brisk, bitter current of air rushed in like an attacking ghost, bringing with it tiny icicles that threatened to cut into them. Snow began to cake the walls and posts, filling in the corners first then covering the floor. The fire in the hearth could not long beat back the elements and was soon extinguished. The fire that had engulfed the walls, on the other hand, continued to burn all around them. If left unattended, the fire would consume the entire building.

Paul's mind raced with jumbled thoughts as his addled brain worked through the problem. What he knew was the monastery was under attack, but by whom, he could not say. Nor did he know why. From his studies, he knew the old man and the monastery had made enemies over the years, but he could not recall any who would want to attack in such a violent fashion. And heaven only knew how they could extinguish the fire that was fast building into a raging inferno around them.

Paul took a step toward the hole that had once been the building's front entrance then suddenly stopped.

A shadow emerged through the haze.

A big shadow cast by an all too familiar form.

It can't be, was the only thought that raced through Paul's mind as he froze in place. *How did he find me?*

Standing in the smashed opening stood the butcher who called himself the absolute ruler of Eritrea, General Kaseem Abdelkrim.

The Cobra.

Paul's nightmare came true.

The Cobra had come for him.

Decked out in a thick animal hide, General Abdelkrim stepped into the holy place, snow caked on his thick boots. He stood tall, hands on his hips as he looked around the room.

Paul was unable to move, paralyzed by the sight before him. He didn't know what to do or say. All he knew for certain was the Cobra had now tracked him down like an animal. Fear rooted Paul to the spot.

"Are you telling me this is the fabled holy place of the scriptures I've heard so much about?" Abdelkrim shouted to no one in particular. "Can this be the place where the sheep in the valley believe the rebellion against me will rise up?" The Cobra laughed. "Pathetic!"

Paul's muscles relaxed. Realization hit him. Abdelkrim hadn't followed him to the holy place after all.

He's not after me. Perhaps he's after the secrets of the Eyes of Judgment! I can't...I can't let that happen!

Paul had faced the general before and lost—lost everything. The Cobra was a strong man and a formidable fighter, and time had no doubt not changed that fact. He had beaten Paul soundly and dropped him into the desert to die a slow, torturous death for no other reason than it amused him.

Paul, on the other hand, had changed considerably since their last encounter. He had learned how to fight and how to protect himself. Plus, there was now the Eyes of Judgment, not that he yet knew how to use them or what they could really do.

Abdelkrim stepped through the opening alone, but Paul felt certain his soldiers would not be far behind. He doubted Abdelkrim had made the perilous journey to Emba Soira by himself. But then again...

Abdelkrim's gaze fell upon the old man, who seemed to watch the intruder with great interest. It was a silent and mental battle of the wills, with Paul watching on with trepidation.

The old man appeared a little wobbly, but perhaps only Paul could tell. To an outsider he almost certainly looked perfectly calm. A small trickle of blood ran from a cut on his forehead, a gift from the Cobra's abrupt entrance. Paul knew his teacher would fight the honorable fight until his last breath, but he also knew the general. He was powerful and would fight dirty.

Paul stepped forth and positioned himself between Abdelkrim and his teacher.

"You?" the general said, clearly surprised to see the man he had left for dead still among the living.

"Me," Paul said, trying to sound confident in the face of a mass murderer who had already bested him once before.

"You!" Abdelkrim shouted.

With a guttural scream, Paul launched himself at his enemy. The attack was clumsy, unthinking and slow, emotion fueling his movements. Paul's heart burned for vengeance for those the Cobra had already murdered.

The battle was lost before it had even begun.

Abdelkrim dealt with Paul just as he had on their previous encounter: with a massive backward punch that sent him flying across the room where he crashed against the burning wall.

Paul screamed in pain, but quickly recovered his footing.

"I know not how you escaped with your life, American," Abdelkrim snarled. "I was obviously too merciful with you. That is a mistake I shall not make again."

Paul and the Cobra ran toward one another, meeting in the center of the burning room.

The Cobra swung first, but Paul sidestepped the punch. Paul landed a hard punch to the gut that staggered the Cobra, but only for a second. Recovering quickly, he placed a succession of quick jabs to Paul's face, bloodying his nose. Paul wiped away the blood and flung it toward the floor. It sizzled in the fire.

"I see you've grown some teeth, little serpent," Abdelkrim said. "That will make killing you so much the sweeter this time."

"You may find me full of surprises," Paul said.

"We'll see."

"Come and get it, you bastard!"

The Cobra launched into a powerful attack, each blow more painful than the one before as he mercilessly pummeled his opponent. Body shot followed gut punch followed a smack to the head.

Paul gave plenty back, but in the end he was outmatched by his opponent's mass, muscle, and sheer brutality. On some level, he was still holding back, pulling his punches. The Cobra did not share that weakness.

Another backhand—the Cobra's signature move—sent Paul crashing once again into the far wall with such force the wood cracked and splintered on impact.

Paul dropped to his hands and knees. He was shaken, but miraculously remained conscious. His vision blurred as tiny suns exploded behind his eyes, threatening to take him completely out of the fight.

Don't pass out! Don't pass out! Don't pass out! Paul thought.

Through sheer force of will, he managed to keep himself stable. The old man was going to need his help. He might be a master of several fighting styles and he was certainly not frail or helpless, but he was still an elderly man and the Cobra was much younger, stronger, and far more ruthless.

Or so Paul believed.

He looked up to see the old man move across the room, agile like a cat in his prime. Then the old man was airborne as he leapt at the invader. He landed a well-placed kick to Abdelkrim's chest, staggering the brute of a man. The old man landed in a crouch, his form textbook perfect.

"Impressive," Abdelkrim said with a smile, a hand rubbing against his chest. "I did not think you had it in you, old man."

"Your coming here was foreseen, serpent, but you are too late," the old man said. "The secrets of our divine scriptures will remain forever hidden from the likes of you."

The Cobra's face contorted in abject rage, then morphed into a sinister smile. "Then I have no further use for you, do I?"

"Do your worst, serpent," the old man said, standing his ground.

"If you insist!"

General Abdelkrim's first punch was wide and easily telegraphed. The old man sidestepped it. The second punch mirrored the first: wide, predictable and effortlessly avoided.

Exactly as planned.

The general's third punch was a haymaker. Putting all of his strength into one massive blow, Abdelkrim delivered a powerful punch that caught the old man on the side of the head. The impact echoed off the walls, along with the audible crack of bone bouncing off bone.

Much as his student had a moment earlier, the old man slammed hard into the far wall then dropped to the floor in a heap, clearly injured and possibly worse.

Get moving, Paul!

Paul rushed to his teacher's side. He felt for a pulse and let out a breath when he found one. It was faint, but the old man still lived. Blood smeared the wall behind him. The old man bled from his head wound, his breathing shallow. Paul knew that if he didn't get his friend some help fast, he was a goner.

The question was, where would he go to find help on top of a mountain surrounded by an invading army?

Sanderson men have to be strong.

His father was right. That was not something he said often, but since coming to Africa and learning of his parents' death, Paul started to see things in a different light. The world was not how he imagined it to be. It never was. There were dangers out there, enemies to stand against, injustices to fight. After years of searching, he could finally see the truth.

Sanderson men need to be strong.

Yes we do, Father.

The boy needs discipline.

The boy has found it.

He needs to grow up.

Paul had become a man now. Hopefully a man a father would be proud of.

Paul stood and faced his enemy. "You bastard," he said. His voice was calm and even, but intense anger burned within his soul. For the first time in his life, he was prepared to kill a man with his own two hands if necessary.

Abdelkrim laughed at the young American who stood before him. He was clearly in no mood for mercy.

"The old man is finished," the Cobra said. "His fate is one you shall now share."

"Not today."

Abdelkrim laughed again.

Paul squared off against the Cobra. Although stronger now than when they first encountered one another at the aid camp, Paul was not yet a skilled hand-to-hand combatant. His lessons were only just beginning when the attack came. There was still much for him to learn before he would be ready to take on an opponent of the Cobra's strength and skill.

But Paul was angry and on the field of battle, anger would count against him.

The Cobra took a swing.

Paul dodged it, but only by centimeters. He felt the air of it as it flashed past. He retaliated and landed a punch to the Cobra's mouth. Anger, and perhaps fear, caused his form to falter, but his aim was true.

Abdelkrim retreated a step as he spat blood from his newly busted lip.

Paul shook his hand and cursed. The impact of knuckles on teeth hurt like hell.

The Cobra smiled again, his teeth stained crimson. "You are stronger than before. More disciplined. It will please me greatly to kill you where you stand."

Paul closed his hands into fists and stood his ground.

The Cobra attacked with a swiftness that matched his namesake. The first shot hit Paul in the midsection and he nearly dropped to his knees. Somehow he managed not to vomit all over the floor.

The second shot connected with Paul's face and he tasted blood.

Despite his righteous anger, Paul was clearly outmatched. His opponent fought hard and he fought to win. The Cobra was powerful, older, more experienced, and a very skilled combatant. He also used his size to his advantage.

Paul spat blood but did not back down.

The Cobra rushed him.

It was not a tactic Paul had anticipated and he was caught completely off guard. The Cobra grabbed him in a big bear hug that lifted him off the floor. Using his size, the Cobra slammed Paul's back into the wall, shattering the burning wood on impact. Both men crashed through the wall and fell into the adjoining room.

Paul kicked himself free of the Cobra's grasp and rolled out of the big man's reach. He took a second to catch his breath, which was no easy feat with the thick smoke filling the monastery.

Abdelkrim didn't give him time to think. He rushed Paul and landed a haymaker that dropped the American back to the floor.

Paul rolled out of the Cobra's reach and got to his feet. Blood ran from his nose, across his lips and down his chin.

"Ready to give up," Paul joked, hoping humor would hide his fear.

"Never!" Abdelkrim pressed the attack again.

Paul held his own, but it was becoming painfully clear once again he was outmatched, outclassed, and outgunned. He could perhaps hold his own a little longer but the odds were in the Cobra's favor. The end was drawing near, he feared.

Abdelkrim threw another punch, connected again, and the world around Paul Sanderson went blurry.

He fell through the hole in the wall and dropped to the floor, but this time did not bounce back up as quickly. He bled from the nose and mouth, his right eye beginning to swell from the crushing blows. But the anger still burned within him. He was down but not yet out. He was not willing to give up, not with so much at stake.

It can't end now...like this, Paul thought.

"Now I will finish this," the Cobra said, moving in for the kill.

Paul's eyes desperately darted back and forth, searching the room. He needed a weapon, something that would help even the odds, even if only slightly. That's when he spotted a broken piece of timber to his left near the fallen body of the old man. It was sharpened to a point at one end—the perfect weapon.

He grabbed it, gripped it tight, and held it in front of him. Paul put all his remaining strength into one last surge and attacked with all the ferocity of a cornered mountain lion. The jagged wood in his hand, he swung hard at the general's head. He heard a soft, squishing sound immediately followed by his enemy howling in pain.

The Cobra flailed backward, his hands flying up to cover his damaged right eye. Blood streamed down his face from where a piece of the timber was embedded in the eye socket. The Cobra was wounded, perhaps evening the battle somewhat, but Paul feared that, like any other wild animal, it would only make him more dangerous.

The Cobra yanked the large splinter from his eye and with a scream of rage tossed it aside. "You gnat!" he shouted in anger. "I will crush you like the bug you are!"

On unsteady feet, Paul backpedaled.

Despite his injury, Abdelkrim moved with amazing speed for one of such size. Even blinded in one eye, he found his enemy with ease and grabbed hold. He pulled Paul into a bear hug so powerful Paul thought he would snap in two. The Cobra squeezed harder.

Paul's bones cracked.

"You have defied me far too long, infidel! This ends now!" Abdelkrim said.

Paul struggled in his clutches, but could not break the big man's hold on him. Doubt began to cloud his mind. He closed his eyes tight in the vain hope he could shut out the pain. It failed.

Another rib snapped.

It's impossible, Paul thought. *It's over. All is lost.*

"No!" The voice burst from Paul Sanderson as though the word was alive. From somewhere deep inside, a familiar fiery sensation grew until every part of him felt ready to spontaneously combust.

His eyes snapped open!

Paul Sanderson screamed as though about to rupture.

Suddenly, the Eyes of Judgment exploded into being as if they had a life of their own. A fireball blossomed off of his chest, forcing the Cobra to release his grip, freeing him from his clutches.

The fiery emanation sent Abdelkrim staggering backward, bumping into the already broken wall then collapsed to his knees.

With the Eyes on his chest burning with fierce intensity, Paul strode toward his kneeling enemy. Whatever was happening to him he could only speculate, but he knew this new power gave him an advantage he did not have before. He pressed forward while the Eyes of Judgment spewed forth strange mystical energies like a geyser.

Determined, the Cobra pushed himself off the floor so he could stare Paul in the face. "I..." he grunted in pain as the fervent tendrils wrapped around him. "I don't know how you are capable of this, but...I will not fall to the likes of you. Never!"

Clearly pushing through the pain, Abdelkrim attacked, forcing his way through the energies emanating from the Eyes of Judgment.

Encircled by flame, the two warriors grappled, face-to-face, each staring into the eyes of the other, neither giving an inch, neither willing to back down.

From the corner of his eye, Paul saw the old man flinch as he watched the battle. Paul hoped beyond hope his friend was all right because he feared the worst.

The Eyes of Judgment burst forth with evermore energy, flames circling them both with an electrical ferocity the sounds of which scared Paul. He had no idea what was happening, nor how to control this incredible power he now possessed, but he pressed forward, hoping it would be enough to vanquish his enemy.

For some reason, the energy of the Eyes seemed to focus on the Cobra's head. The intense heat from the flames—though Paul didn't feel it—cauterized the wound to the Cobra's right eye, stopping the bleeding and turning the eye a milky white as the skin around the eye socket bubbled and burned.

"What...what are you doing to me?" the Cobra muttered. It was the first time Paul had sensed fear within his enemy.

Behind the blind eye, an uncontrollable mystical storm raged.

Suddenly, a white energy force shot free from the Cobra's eye, lancing out in defiance to the energies of the Eyes of Judgment. The beam slammed into the Judgment Stare almost as though it was fighting against it. "What...is...happening...to me?" the Cobra shouted as ribbons of energy lanced around him, stabbing at him the way a snake attacks its prey.

"I feel...I feel power...building inside me!" the Cobra screamed. "Power!"

Paul had no idea of the extent of the power he now possessed. All he could do was press forward, his actions fueled by adrenalin alone.

As the battle raged, their grappling increased in fury, and the energies building around them became unstable, threatening to overwhelm them both.

Paul's power and the Cobra's power merged together—

—and quickly reached critical mass.

The resulting explosion sent both combatants flying across the room in opposite directions.

Paul landed hard, tried to recover, tried to...

Darkness.

~ Chapter 13 ~

Every inch of Paul Sanderson hurt.

He floated alone in the dark, neither falling nor flying.

Instead, he simply hung aloft while surrounded by nothingness. It should have been peaceful, but...

You need to wake up, son!

Paul forced open his eyes a slit.

Darkness greeted him.

Wake up!

His eyes shot open and he sat up hard, coughing away the taste of smoke and blood. Slowly, carefully, he pushed himself onto his knees then to his feet. He was wobbly but managed to stay upright. Barely.

He stood alone in a snowdrift outside. All around him lay the wreckage and burning debris of the monastery he had called home for the past several months. What little of it that was left was engulfed in flames.

There was no sign of Abdelkrim or his men. Had the blast killed his enemy? He hoped so, but there was no way of knowing for sure. Without such knowledge, justice would, unfortunately, be left unfulfilled.

The old man was nowhere in sight. The last time Paul had seen him, he was injured, watching the battle. Paul took a step forward, shivering against the cold wind that wrapped around him. Even the intense flame of his erstwhile home wouldn't keep him warm for long.

"My son..." a weak, familiar voice called.

Paul spun around, a bit too quickly, his vision blurring briefly. The old man lay in another snowdrift a little ways in front of him. He was wounded, terribly so. His left leg was broken and bent at an odd angle. Even at this distance, Paul could tell his master's breathing was shallow, almost non-existent.

"Master!" Paul shouted as he ran to the old man's side.

"There isn't much time left," the old man said in a hoarse whisper. "We must hurry. I must impart to you as much information as time will allow."

"No," Paul said firmly. "We need to get you off this mountain. You called me a savior once. Now it is time I saved you."

"No. It is far too late for that. I have always known that I will die on this mountain. I accepted my fate years ago. I am content." He spluttered, blood curdling over his chin. "The prophecy has been fulfilled." Tears formed in Paul's eyes. He knew the end was near for his dear friend and mentor.

"Come. Sit," the old man said. His breathing was forced, labored, but he was clearly determined to stay alive long enough to say his piece. Paul found a singed pillow nearby and placed it behind his fallen master, then sat next to his friend and listened.

The old man steadied himself. "This power that you now possess is not a curse, but a gift, my son," he wheezed then stopped to catch his breath. "You have been granted the power to cleanse mankind of evil in all its forms. All save those with the most powerful of wills will be affected by the Judgment Stare. The power is greater than any one man. In turn, the power, memories and even the personality of its bearer can be transferred to someone worthy if the bearer's time is at an end. The Eyes of Judgment must carry on to do its work."

"You mean...if I'm dying?"

"Yes," the old man said and coughed. "This is not a gift that is bestowed lightly, my son, as you know. Only one who is truly worthy can ever wield the Eyes of Judgment."

The old man tapped a bony finger against Paul's chest. "That man is you. I knew it from the moment I met you."

"I'm glad one of us did," Paul joked. "You and Sam were the only ones who believed. I'm still not sure what to make of it all."

The old man coughed and his body seized.

Paul held his friend's hand tight, afraid to let go. His master was dying and there was nothing he could do to save him.

"You...you will carry on. You will take the Eyes of Judgment into the...the world and right that which has gone so, so wrong." The old man's voice weakened and was now barely audible above the wind. "The prophecy has...been...fulfilled."

The old man's head slumped and rolled to one side.

He was gone.

With so much still left unsaid.

Paul held his friend's hand in his for a long time until eventually the fire went out and the creeping cold of the mountain top began reclaiming its territory. With the monastery now consumed, there was nothing left to fight back the frigid conditions.

The holy man of Emba Soira was dead.

Paul Sanderson blamed himself. *Another soul I could not save. Like Judy. Like the aid camp workers. Like my parents.*

Grief has a way of helping even the most stubborn of souls make life-changing decisions. At that moment, Paul Sanderson made the decision to return home to Metro City.

It was time.

Are you ready? On this occasion, the voice he heard echoing in his head did not belong to his father, but to the old man.

Paul said his final goodbyes as he used a plank of wood to dig a rudimentary grave for his friend and mentor atop the snowy mountaintop he'd called home. A simple headstone made from yet another remaining plank of wood marked the grave of the man who had become his dearest friend. A man who had given him so much and asked for nothing in return save to use his newfound abilities for good. To help people, as Paul had always wanted to.

Paul stood in prayer over the snow-covered lump of ground where his friend lay buried. He knew nature would soon reclaim the mountaintop, that the wreckage and grave would quickly disappear as though it had never been there at all. This was the fate of the man who had been more of a father to him than any he had ever known. Tears streamed down Paul's face. He had discovered so much on Emba Soira. About the world, about life. About himself. And he had also made the greatest of enemies in the process. His one fear was that General Abdelkrim—the Cobra—had somehow escaped death just as he had done. If that proved to be the case, he knew their paths would cross again and that next time, justice *would* be served.

Despite the pain and loss he had endured over the last year of his life, Paul had also found something he had been searching for for far longer. He found a purpose. The path before him was more clear than it had ever been before.

At that moment, he knew what must be done.

"Thank you," he finally said to his friend and teacher.

Scrounging amongst the wreckage of the monastery, Paul found some rags that, when wrapped around him, served to keep himself warm, and a goatskin gourd, which he grabbed and slung over his shoulder. Then, with one final look at the destruction around him, Paul started the long trek down the mountain.

He didn't look back.

* * * * * *

Paul's first stop was to visit an old friend.

Once he reached the base of the mountain, he was tempted to get away, to escape Eritrea and all its pain for good, but he couldn't. After everything Sam had done for him, Paul could not leave Africa without saying goodbye. He also needed to tell him all that had transpired. He owed his friend that.

The long journey from Emba Soira to Sam's home proved as drawn-out and treacherous as before, especially so as he was now dressed only in rags and had no food, save what he was able to scrounge along the way. Thankfully, he had the water in his gourd procured from the mountainside spring, but that wouldn't last long. Yet, he was also stronger now, both in body and spirit, and would not easily give in to the elements as he might have done before. He had changed.

Sam was outside playing with his daughters when Paul walked into view.

Giggling, Huey, Lewey, and Dewey ran toward him and leaped into their Uncle Paul's outstretched arms. They were as excited to see him as he was them.

"How ya doing, kiddos?" he shouted as they tumbled to the sand.

After a few moments playing with the girls, Paul walked over to his brother. They shook hands.

"The girls have gotten so big," Paul said.

Sam beamed with pride. "My little flowers are growing like weeds, eh?"

Paul enveloped him in a big bear hug. "How are you, Sam?"

"It is good to see you," Sam said in that deep husky voice Paul had missed. "You have changed. You are bigger, *more* somehow."

"Yes," Paul said. "You were right, Sam. All this time, you and the old man were right. I never knew, never believed." Tears began welling in his eyes.

"I know," Sam said sadly. "I know all."

Paul rocked backwards. "How? How could you know anything?"

"Do you still not understand, my friend? The prophecy! It has been fulfilled. Your presence here, the fact that you have changed so—all has been fulfilled. All is thus known to me."

Paul was unable to stem the flow of tears. "I couldn't help him, Sam. He died in my arms. Abdelkrim killed him. All that I've learned, all the power I now have and...and I couldn't save him."

"It was not your destiny to save him, therefore this guilt you feel is unwarranted and unworthy of you," Sam said matter-of-factly. "All is as was prophesied. All is as it should be. Take heart in that. All is as it should be."

The tears stopped. Paul knew deep down Sam was right. Despite the horror and pain and sadness, all *was* as it should be. He knew that to be true. All he could do now was move forward and continue with what he started, to make good on the promise and power given to him by the prophecy. By the old man.

"This...prophecy. Will I ever learn who wrote it? Where it came from?"

"No one knows," Sam replied. "It is long lost in the mists of time."

Paul bowed his head, not knowing what to make of it all.

"What will you do next?" Sam asked after some moments of silence.

"My battle with Abdelkrim taught me something," Paul said. "That I still have so much to learn. I need to master hand-to-hand combat in all its forms. If I am to use my abilities to cleanse the world of evil, I need to learn how to formulate plans, battle tactics, investigative procedures. To understand the psychology of the criminal mind." He took a deep breath. "I am not yet ready to return to Metro City. My journey has only just begun."

"When will you go?" Sam asked softly.

"As soon as possible." Paul looked down at the rags covering him. "I hate to impose on your kindness once again, but...I can't make the journey dressed like this."

"Indeed."

"And I just couldn't leave Africa without saying goodbye to you and Mala and the girls and to thank you for all you've done for me. You and your family...you saved my life, but I think, in all the ways that matter, you also helped save my soul. For that, I will be forever grateful."

"Stay for dinner," Sam said.

"I don't want to impose any further than I already have."

"Nonsense. Mala loves to cook and the girls are overjoyed at your return. Stay tonight. Rest. Your journey can wait a few hours more."

Paul finally nodded in acquiescence. In truth, he couldn't say no to such a dear friend.

The evening was filled with laughter. Paul regaled the family with tales from his time atop Emba Soira, mostly the embarrassing stuff that ended with him either falling into the pond fed by the spring or with him busting his buns on the ice. The girls giggled with glee with each fall and slip. Paul knew his audience and played up the humor to the hilt, even going so far as to act out some of the more interesting stories.

Mala prepared an incredible meal and they ate with gusto. No offense to the old man, but this was the best meal Paul had eaten since the last time he had stayed with Sam and his family.

Dinner was followed by more stories and laughter, but as with all good things, it eventually reached an end. Sam and Mala tucked the girls in for the night, but not before each child took a turn hugging Uncle Paul. Once the girls were settled, Mala also said goodnight and offered Paul a hug as well. He kissed her cheek and thanked her for everything.

Grabbing a bottle of wine from a locked cabinet, Sam led Paul outside where they once again sat on the wooden bench. They toasted one another and the journey ahead while watching the stars dance above.

"The desert sure is beautiful at night," Paul said. "During the day, it is hot, blinding, and inhospitable. But at night, when the air cools and the stars come out, it's actually enchanting."

"The desert sand gets in your blood," Sam said.

"Not to mention every crack and crevice of your body." Paul laughed.

Sam smiled in reply.

"This...today has been wonderful," Paul said. "Thank you. I needed to laugh after...after..."

"You are always welcome here, my brother," Sam said. "You know this."

"I do. I also know that I must keep moving. I will leave at daybreak."

Sam nodded. "Then, before you go, I have a present for you."

"What?" Paul said, stunned.

Sam held out a small towel wrapped around something roughly the size of Paul's open hand. "It was the least I could do."

"I don't need anything, Sam. You and your family have little enough as it is, and I've already taken too much."

"Enough," Sam said. "Look."

Paul unwrapped it. He smiled as he held up his father's watch. "I was wondering what happened to this. Where did you find it?"

"It was here," Sam said, "beside your cot. You must have dropped it while packing."

Paul held up the Rolex. "Thank you. This means a lot to me, more than I ever realized."

The two friends sat together and talked for hours until even Sam admitted it was time to turn in. He still had to work in the fields come the morning and he was no longer a young man who could brave the desert without at least a few hours rest. He offered Paul the same cot he had slept on the last time he was with them.

It was the best night's sleep Paul had gotten in months.

* * * * * *

When Paul woke with the dawn, he was not surprised to see his friend was already up and waiting for him, presumably to say one last goodbye.

"I should have known I couldn't sneak away so easily," Paul said with a smile.

"No, you couldn't."

Paul shook his friend's hand, then took the small tribesman in his arms in a hearty hug. "Thank you again for everything you've done for me. I...I'm not sure I'll ever be back here. I may never see you again."

"All is as it should be," Sam said. "Take heart in that."

Paul smiled. "I will. I do."

And with that, with one last smile, he turned and started on his next journey.

"Stay safe, my friend," Sam called out.

Paul did not look back.

~ Chapter 14 ~

Paul Sanderson planned to travel the world.

First, however, he had to get out of Africa in one piece. Vast areas of the continent were as dangerous as Eritrea had been, if not more so. Savage civil wars dragged on in many surrounding countries. Famine and disease reigned supreme in yet others. And warlords and wild beasts still intended on wreaking harm upon him at every turn.

He had to get out of Africa as soon as possible.

Or sooner.

Paul needed to learn everything. And he needed to find those that could best teach him the skills he required.

After leaving Sam's hut, Paul walked across the desert and back into the horn of Africa. He had learned a bit about the area from his time working at the aid camp. Before heading toward the nearest airstrip to barter for a plane ride, he stopped by the camp. All that remained was scorched earth where the camp and everything in it had stood. Only the freshly churned dirt marked the mass grave where General Abdelkrim's men had buried their victims before torching what remained of the camp.

There were no survivors that he was aware of.

Except him.

Whether or not the Cobra had survived, he knew the general's men were still out there and still posed a threat to him. Avoiding their patrols wasn't easy, but he managed to stay out of trouble on his way to the airfield.

Two days later, he arrived at the airstrip where the camp's pilot, Major Hawkins, used to transport supplies and the wounded in and out. As he entered the grounds, he briefly wondered if Hawkins had survived. He made his way slowly and cautiously to the strip's sole hangar, if it could be called that, and nearly bumped into a man exiting the building—Major Hawkins.

"Hawkins," Paul said with a few tears. "I didn't dare hope, but...here you are."

Hawkins let loose with a warm laugh and grabbed Paul in a hearty embrace. "I could say the same for you. When I came back from my run there was nothing...no one left. I almost ran smack bang into General Abdelkrim's battalion, but managed to hide while his men buried the dead. So many bodies...so many..." He choked up.

"I know," Paul said softly, his head hanging low. "I was there. I saw it all. I couldn't stop them."

"But you survived," Hawkins said. "How came you alive in this hellhole of a place?"

"It'd take too long to tell you the story and I really don't have the time or inclination to go through all that again. I need to get out of here. Out of Africa. Can you help me?"

"Sure, sure, fella. Let me just get some supplies from the bar over there and we'll be off. Your timing couldn't be more perfect. Plane's full of fuel and ready to go. We can even make it to Europe if we really push it."

The tiny airfield was little more than a patch of dirt long enough to land a small aircraft on. That was all it took for a smuggler's airfield to spring to life. A tiny hut had been built off to the side of the small hangar to serve as an office and bar. It wasn't a local hangout. Hawkins related the only people drowning their sorrows in that bar were either pilots or people running to or from something.

Twenty minutes later, Paul sat in the co-pilot's chair of a Fairchild C-119B. Paul hadn't seen a plane this old outside of a museum or classic television series, but Hawkins guaranteed that the "Ol' Flying Boxcar" would get them where they were going.

He was right.

Once he was back on good old terra firma in the south of Spain, Paul picked a direction and started walking until he faded into the morning fog and vanished.

* * * * * *

The next two years were a blur.

After leaving Africa, Paul fell off the grid and disappeared. From the deserts of Africa to the cold foggy mornings of Europe, he made his way across the continent by plane, foot, car, bicycle, and even a couple of horse-drawn carts. On those nights when there were available lodgings nearby, he would check in under an assumed name to make sure nobody would be able to track his movements. He was determined that no one, not Abdelkrim or anyone else, would know where he was or what he intended to do.

He realized if he was to make use of his newfound abilities and fulfill his destiny, he needed to learn more. He needed to find the best there was and absorb from them all he could. That meant finding teachers willing to train an outsider. Eventually, he connected with those who would help him. All across the continent, Paul learned multiple martial arts disciplines from various teachers while he picked up battle tactics from others. Other skills he picked up along the way included athletics, strength training, breath control, gymnastics, basic medical training, code-breaking, deductive reasoning, hand/eye coordination, chemistry, lock-picking, safe-cracking, and psychology. Anything remotely useful to his future life, he absorbed with an intensity he had never shown during his college years.

Even as he acquired these new skills, Paul continued to work and train himself to control the Eyes of Judgment. Of all the studies he had undertaken thus far, this was the most difficult to master. Without the old man to train and guide him, he found it almost impossible to acquire the control over the Eyes that he needed to make his future mission a success. Gradually, however, as the months dragged on and on, he was able get better and better at activating the Judgment Stare. He knew then that with more time and further concentration and meditation, full control over this power would be his. He just had to have faith and apply the teachings of his sadly lost master.

As months became years, Paul was more confident in his abilities than ever, but there was still much to learn and there were miles to go before he was ready. He now found himself in the English countryside on the grounds of an ancient castle that had long fallen into disrepair and was being used as a retreat for those seeking spiritual guidance. Paul spent some months there, honing his meditation skills and learning to be patient. And to have faith.

After two months spent there amongst the monks in prayer, he finally came to understand how the Eyes of Judgment worked and how to activate them. True, they often had a life of their own, and sometimes would appear when not bidden, Paul found he could now control them and use them as the old man had intended. Now it truly was time to return home and begin his life's work.

It had been over a year since he heard his father's voice nagging at him from beyond. As much as he hated to admit it, sometimes he missed the old man's griping.

He accepted a ride from a farmer delivering his crops to the market. It was a journey of some hours, but it did him well traveling through the gorgeous English countryside. Rolling green hills, beautiful blue streams, oaks, elms, and birches all around him. It made for a stark, and highly desirable, change from that of Africa. He much preferred it.

A few hours later, Paul found himself just outside London.

~ Chapter 15 ~

In many ways, London reminded Paul of home.

As he walked down a busy London thoroughfare, the hustle and bustle of one of the world's grandest and busiest cities made him feel homesick. London and Metro City were both giant monuments to human endurance with their towers of glass and steel reaching heavenward. The climate was different, certainly more rain-soaked for much of the year in London, but after all that time in the desert, the cool, damp air was a welcome change. His studies were now at an end. He was stronger, fitter, more sure of himself than he had ever been in his life. And he had mastered the powers of the Eyes of Judgment. His stay in London had been memorable and restful, but the time had finally come for the prodigal son to return home and begin his quest. Metro City was waiting for him. After a full day spent training, Paul strolled along the street enjoying the crisp night air, a thick overcoat cinched around his waist. From the outside, he looked like any other well-dressed gentleman oblivious to the dangers around him.

As Paul passed a narrow alleyway, he heard someone shout, "Hey! Come here!"

The thug reached out and grabbed Paul, manhandling him as he threw his intended victim back first against the rough brick wall.

Paul was startled but quickly recovered. Before he could make a move, the man who attacked him pointed a gun directly between his eyes. "Hi there," the man said with a menacing sneer.

Paul did as instructed. He stood still, his body rigid, his training now coming to the fore, ready to strike when the opportunity presented itself. This was certainly not the first gun to ever be pointed at him. It was certainly not the first time he had faced death nor was it likely to be his last.

"In the alley, mate," the thug said.

Able to do nothing more at the present, Paul complied. The thug was a short, sturdy man wearing a peaked cap with bushy red hair and sideburns sticking out of it that appeared to have not been touched by either shampoo or a comb in days, possibly weeks. As they both shuffled into the alley, Paul saw there were ample ways for him to disarm the gunman, to end it there and then, but something inside him told him to wait. A gut instinct he had learned to heed.

The attacker looked menacing enough as he waved his gun about. He was clearly on something, some drug that had given him an added dose of courage while making him shaky and uneven on his feet. His bloodshot eyes were evidence enough of this, the pupils like pinpoints.

"C'mon, gimme your wallet and watch," the thug said in a thick Irish brogue, "and be quick about it. Max Horton doesn't like ta be kept waitin'."

* * * * * *

Leena gasped when she heard Paul mention that name. "Max? On drugs? A petty thief? I can't believe it. It's horrible."

"It's not a past he's proud of, as you can well imagine," Paul explained. "He had fallen into addiction in his teens and, as he grew older, turned to a life of petty crime to feed his growing cravings. Who knows where he might have ended up if he hadn't bumped into Paul Sanderson that fateful night?"

* * * * * *

LONDON - FIVE YEARS EARLIER

Paul handed over his wallet to the assailant.

"Why are you doing this?" he asked as Max snatched the wallet from his hand. "I sense within you a yawning chasm. You don't really want to do this, do you?"

"Shut up!" Max shouted. He was agitated, flailing his gun around with one hand while the other rifled through the wallet. There were only a handful of bills in there along with a fake ID and an Oyster card that allowed him access to the tubes.

Paul stared at Max, emotionless.

"C'mon, mate, I said cough up your watch as well."

Paul let out a breath. "You don't want to do this."

"Don't gimme that," Max said around a greedy smile. "This watch will fetch me quite a few quid. Tonight, I drink the good stuff. Who knows, maybe I'll even buy a drink or two for one of the fetching lasses that rarely give a poor bloke like me a second glance. I'm sure a rich, good-lookin' feller like yerself wouldn't know what that's like now, would ya?"

"You'd be surprised," Paul said.

"Enough stallin'! Fork over the watch!"

Slowly, he pulled back his sleeve to reach for his father's Rolex. Instead of removing the expensive timepiece as instructed, Paul moved with lightning fast speed and snatched the gun out of his assailant's hand before Max even realized the gun was no longer there.

Startled, Max backpedaled as panic clearly set in.

The man he had no doubt believed to be an easy mark took a menacing step toward him. Fear grew on Max Horton's face.

Instead of attacking, Paul slipped the gun into his coat pocket. He looked at Max, never breaking eye contact. "You are in great pain," he said. "I can bring you the inner peace you crave. I can force you to come to terms with your sins or you can accept it voluntarily. Which will it be?"

"What...what are you talking about?" Max said as he tried to get away. He slipped trying to back away and fell on his rear.

"I can show you a new path," Paul said, still moving slowly toward Max.

Max's eyes grew wide as Paul's chest began to glow.

The Eyes of Judgment appeared. The power took no heed of clothing and would appear whenever needed. The light shone bright, crackling with mystical energy.

"I can give you judgment for your past sins or" —Paul smiled— "I can offer you redemption."

"Stay away from me, man!" Max shouted, trying to shield his eyes from the bright light.

"That is the one thing I cannot do," Paul said.

Max screamed out for help. "I'll not be taken by ye're wraith. Ye cannot have me this day."

"Make your choice," Paul said with finality. No longer was he the average American tourist, the scrawny youth who didn't know his place in the world, the young man searching for answers. In his place stood a dread avenger of justice, with a voice so deep and menacing it echoed off the brick walls surrounding them. The echo only added to the ghost-like quality he exuded.

"I...I can't!"

"Then I shall choose for you."

Max screamed like a man who knew he was about to die.

The Eyes of Judgment burst to life, flames reaching forth to mete out their ultimate justice. Paul let Max have it with the full strength of the Judgment Stare.

The Eyes' energy enveloped Max fully. He howled in pain as ribbons of energy danced across his skin. Paul noticed even through the energy sizzling about them that the hairs all over Max's body stood on end. The pain Max experienced must have been intense, almost certainly unlike anything he'd felt before.

Max's body went limp and he crumpled to his knees as though willing himself to die.

Until, as suddenly as it began, the power was gone. And with it, the howls of pain.

Max, on his knees, sobbed uncontrollably as wisps of residual smoke roiled off of him.

Paul stood over him, power still radiating from him.

"Ye're a blasted wraith, ye are!" Max said. "What have you done to me?"

"I have freed you," Paul said softly, as if Max's experience was a common, everyday occurrence. "I showed you the truth. What you do with that truth is now up to you."

"Th...thank you," Max replied. "You...you *have* freed me...brought me back from the abyss. I can feel it. The hunger is gone. My mind...my soul...is mine again. I did not realize what I'd lost...truly lost...until you helped me find myself again."

Smiling, Paul helped the shaky man to his feet.

"N...name's Max," he said.

"I know, you already told me," Paul said with a smile. "I'm Paul. Pleasure to meet you, Max. Can you stand properly?"

He helped Max regain his footing, the latter still a little groggy after his ordeal.

"How on earth did you end up in such a mess, Max?"

Max shuffled, humiliation and shame clouding his features. "It's an old story, mate, and too long and humiliating to tell to you now. But I will tell you...one day."

"You needn't," Paul said. "It's in the past now. Your past. Let it stay there. You're free from that pain forevermore."

"Thank you," Max said again. "But...what did you do to me? What was that...wraith thing that attacked me?"

Paul smiled. "I've never heard it called that before. As to exactly what it is, and what it did for you...like yours, it's a rather long story."

"If you're not going anywhere, I'm ready to hear your long story."

It was there, on an empty street in London's East End, that Max Horton dedicated his life to helping Paul Sanderson with his quest for justice. He later revealed he owed such a debt of gratitude to Paul it could only be repaid with such a lifelong duty.

When Paul left London two days later, bound for Metro City, Max Horton joined him.

* * * * * *

The last time Paul Sanderson saw his family home, he was a teenager. Many arduous years had passed since then.

"It hasn't changed much," he said as he and Max Horton stood outside the entrance to the Sanderson family estate known as Sanderson House. After arriving in Metro City, he had considered calling Simpson to let him know he had returned, but then thought better of it. Paul wanted to surprise his old friend.

He could scarcely believe how nervous he was as he pushed the buzzer.

A few moments later, the door opened and there stood his old family friend.

"Uh, hi there," Paul said.

"May I help you, sir?" Jonathan Simpson, the Sanderson butler, said with his usual formal grace.

"Simpson. It's me. Don't you recognize me?"

The man's eyes grew wide when he did recognize the young man standing before him.

"Master Paul?" Simpson stammered at last.

"It's good to see you," Paul said with a sincere grin.

The normal prim and proper Simpson pulled his charge into an uncharacteristic hug.

"Welcome home, sir," Simpson said. "Welcome home."

They parted and Simpson got his first good look at the man who Paul had since become. He beamed with pride and joy.

"How long will you be staying, sir?" Simpson asked, no doubt recalling Paul's wandering spirit.

"I'm back for good, Simpson."

"Very good, sir," the butler said as if it was just a normal day at the manor.

"There is much work to do."

"So, you'll be joining the family business after all?" Simpson asked, a look of surprise appearing on his face.

"Not exactly, Simpson," Paul said. "I'm starting a new venture. Once we get settled in, I'll tell you about it."

"Very good, sir," Simpson said as he stepped aside to allow Paul entry. "And your friend, sir?"

"Simpson, this is Max Horton," Paul said. "Max is my...uh..."

The two men exchanged a look, shrugged.

"My chauffeur," Paul finally said. "And mechanic."

"Your chauffeur?" Simpson appeared dubious, but did not openly question the statement. "Your mechanic?"

"Yes. Both," Paul confirmed, more assured. "Can you have a room set up for him?"

"Of course," Simpson said, nodding at the newcomer as he walked past carrying luggage. Paul could tell Simpson's guard was up around the new arrival. All through life, the butler had been there to protect Paul wherever possible, and Simpson was now undoubtedly reverting to that habit. He would soon change his opinion on Max, Paul felt. In time, all would become clear to his oldest friend.

"Shall I have your belongings transferred to the master bedroom, sir?" Simpson asked.

Paul's shoulders slumped. He turned to face him. "I...um...I don't think I'm quite ready for that, Simpson. My old room will suffice for now. Perhaps in time..."

"Of course, sir. I understand."

Paul clapped Max on the shoulder. "How about I show you around, give you the nickel tour?"

"That's a coin, right?" Max said with a twinkle in his eye. "Do you rich folks even know what a nickel looks like?" Max chuckled.

"I saw a photo of one once," Paul said with a smirk.

"I'll have the kitchen prepare a small lunch, sir," Simpson said as the two men walked deeper into the mansion.

Paul turned back to him. "Good plan. After lunch we'll get started."

"Sir?"

"There's a lot of work to do, Simpson, and very little time to waste."

* * * * * *

The next few weeks were busy.

Paul used the fortune his parents had left him to begin his mission. With Max's expertise in electronics and engineering, construction soon began on the Lair, a secret command center hidden deep within the core of the great Sanderson home. Once completed, the Lair would become a multi-level structure housed partially on ground level and partially underground, with access through a secret doorway in the library and through multiple discreet entry and exit points scattered throughout the estate. Within the Lair, the various equipment needed to wage a war on crime would be housed. The Lair would be the ultimate crime fighting lab.

But there was one element still missing.

Paul Sanderson's wealth and family name were powerful tools on their own, but the criminal element would see him more as a target than something to fear. And he needed to protect the lives of those around him, such as Simpson and Max. While he didn't care much for his own personal life—he'd lost too much to focus on that—he didn't want his friends or associates to have to face the same dangers twenty four hours a day.

So, Paul had the perfect solution.

"Are you sure about this?" Max asked, holding up a portion of a dark blue and white outfit for Paul to examine.

"Yes," Paul said. "This will only work if I remain anonymous. This can't be tracked back to me or my family's business or name. My parents' legacy has to be protected."

"So you designed a costume?"

"Uniform, Max. And you did that. I merely told you what I was after. Now, tell me all about it."

"Well," Max started, "this outfit will be comfortable as well as protective. It's tear-resistant with a Kevlar-reinforced lining. It might not stop a bullet, but it will slow it down. The cape is a little tougher and should deflect anything but high-powered gunfire. It should also repel most bladed weapons. The pouches in the belt are filled with small gas grenades plus a few accessories that might come in handy out there."

"Excellent," Paul said, smiling.

Max grimaced as he looked over the suit. "But it looks so..."

"That's by design," Paul said, cutting him off. He tapped the chest piece emblazoned in yellow with an emblem resembling the Eyes of Judgment. "I wanted it to look this way. It really harkens back to the heroes of yesteryear that I used to love reading about, both real and imagined. Colorful costumed heroes who saved the world. I always wished that could be me. Now it can be."

Max lifted his cap off his brow and scratched his head. "What do ye plan to call yerself, if you don't mind me asking?"

Paul smiled as he pulled the cowl—resembling the mask Zorro wore, but made of a heavy duty rubber with a faux knot at the back—over his head. It fit perfectly.

"Do you remember what you called me when we first met in London? How you described the Eyes of Judgment?"

Realization gripped Max. "I called it—you—a wraith."

"Exactly. Wraith. The perfect name, don't you think?"

"The Wraith," Max said. "Certainly has a nice ring to it."

"The Wraith sallies forth from this night forward. Metro City beware...judgment is coming!"

~ Chapter 16 ~

Over the next several months, The Wraith cut a mighty swath through Metro City's underworld, earning the nickname of the Dread Avenger. He tackled all crime head-on. Large or small, it didn't matter. He helped the downtrodden, the besieged, and the forgotten in a way the legitimate police couldn't—or wouldn't—even if the Metro PD had not been ravaged by the disease of graft and corruption. Muggers, drug dealers, pimps, arsonists, crooked politicians, unsavory businessmen, and many more—The Wraith knew no boundaries.

The message soon became clear: if you were a criminal, the Dread Avenger of the Underworld was coming for you.

To the public at large, The Wraith was largely a myth, many believing him an invention of the police to frighten criminals. He appeared only to lawbreakers. Even the police force refused to believe in his existence, at least publicly so.

But to others, The Wraith became a symbol of hope and freedom in a city where those commodities were in short supply. No matter what, The Wraith worked to bring justice and lawfulness to a city that had very little time for either. Metro City had fallen on hard times, there was no denying that. The city was strewn with shadowy alleyways that appeared menacing and foreboding.

The Wraith acted as a beacon, burning away the shadows where the scary men lived. His mission was to prove to the citizens of Metro City there was a path back from the brink. Together, they could revitalize their city and save it from those who would destroy it. He would show the one man who ran the city's underworld—crime lord Robert Latham— that a reckoning was close at hand.

As Paul had found out, to the world at large, Latham was a legitimate businessman, involved in a corporation with interests in multiple industries, including the media. To those in the know, however, he was also the head of the largest crime cartel on the Eastern Seaboard. He was the true power in Metro City, and yielded this power to his best advantage. Whatever there was to control in the city, it all led back to him, like a giant spider in an intricate web enveloping all of Metro.

Night after night, The Wraith took down men and women working for Latham, shutting down operations all across the city. From those lieutenants who reported directly to the man himself to the underlings who did not even realize they ultimately reported to him, The Wraith squashed them all. He dismantled Latham's interests with glee while saving—or destroying—as many souls as he could along the way thanks to the power of the Eyes of Judgment. The ultimate fate of those condemned to the Judgment Stare was determined by how great their evil was.

The Wraith was making a dent, but progress was not as swift as he had hoped. He was but one man when all was said and done.

Robert Latham was a powerful man on both sides of the law. He was smart and cunning and knew how to play the game. He understood politics and crime, as they were often two sides of the same coin. Ousting him and his number two man, Charlie Grieco, from Metro City was going to be harder than Paul had first believed, but he was patient. No matter how long it took, he would see justice served.

While The Dread Avenger of the Underworld prowled the rooftops of Metro City by night, Paul Sanderson worked quietly during the daylight hours to help others fight the good fight. He anonymously donated funds and equipment to the police department, backed honest politicians seeking office, funded charity events, safe zones and playgrounds for children all the while studying his enemy. Paul subtly manipulated events from the shadows of anonymity with one goal in mind—the dismantling of Robert Latham's empire until Metro City was no longer under his sway.

Day and night, Paul Sanderson lived the mission until that was all there was for him. He eschewed any semblance of a normal life. Paul had become the mask. The Wraith was all he lived for, all he wanted—needed—to be.

*Maybe after the mission is completed...*he once told himself even though he knew it was a convenient lie.

The mission was always evolving, growing. It would never be finished. There was too much work to be done.

Being The Wraith was his entire existence. He accepted that fact.

And thus, despite the noted concerns of both Jonathan Simpson and Max Horton, Paul Sanderson faded away from the limelight and became a recluse of some renown. Paul

Sanderson sightings had become a game played by Metro City citizens once the press caught wind the heir of one of Metro City's most valued families had returned home after a long absence.

The press had a field day with his homecoming.

Why had he returned? Was Paul reclaiming his family's fortune? Would he appoint himself the head of the Sanderson business empire? Where had Paul Sanderson been all these years? Had he been part of a secret cult before his parents' death? Had the Sanderson's been kidnapped by aliens? These were the questions that assaulted the city—indeed, the country—on a daily basis in the paper, on television and, especially, on the Internet.

When Paul started refusing all requests for interviews and turned down all invitations to social events, it only added to the mythos that erupted around him. His avoidance of the public—for he never ventured out of the grounds of the Sanderson estate save when outfitted as The Wraith at night—only fueled the rampant speculation of what was wrong with him. Over time, the tabloid press, in particular, started a rumor Paul was dying or carried some sort of malicious disease that made headlines elsewhere in the country or the world. Hepatitis. AIDS. Ebola. At one stage or another, Paul Sanderson was afflicted with these and more. Another report claimed the young millionaire had turned the Sanderson mansion into a playground for his tawdry sexual pursuits and had become a modern day Caligula. Yet another posited, and this was his favorite, that Paul Sanderson's body had died and his head was kept in the mansion in a state of suspended animation until cloning proved a viable option to bring him back to life.

Paul laughed off the ridiculous headlines. He soon realized that Simpson and Max were not laughing, however. Not at all.

* * * * * *

As The Wraith's war on crime heated up, Paul Sanderson's life was put on permanent hold.

When he wasn't working in the Lair, he spent his time sitting in his father's study with the heavy curtains drawn, brooding alone in the dark or reading by a low light. He rarely slept more than a couple of hours at a time, when he bothered to sleep at all. He ate even less until Simpson reminded him The Wraith's mission would come to a premature end of he didn't refuel his body and stay healthy. Each morning, Paul returned home battered and bruised, sometimes bleeding, and Simpson and Max would be there to patch him up so he could go out and do it all over again as soon as the sun set.

Simpson once asked Paul if he had a death wish, but was firmly fobbed off. Paul was not willing to discuss the matter any further. He informed Simpson it was The Wraith's mission to save the world. Paul Sanderson need not exist anymore.

"It's yours and Max's mission to keep me safe and sound as much as possible. Keep me going so I can continue with *my* mission." Paul was resolute in his decision.

They were missions constantly at odds with one another. Each needed to be in perfect sync with the other, but they were not. Not even close.

Every evening as the sun set behind the skyscrapers of Metro City, The Wraith suited up for work, popping a couple of pain pills when needed, which was becoming more and more often. The trio had spent the hours before dusk going over the plan to remove Robert Latham from power and thusly release his stranglehold on Metro and her people. The Wraith needed evidence and for that they needed an informant. They had to have someone far enough down the chain of command so as to be relatively easy to turn against their boss and become The Wraith's inside man. The plan was to then convince, forcibly if need be, the informant's boss to turn on their boss and so on all the way up the chain until they reached the frightening spider behind it all. They needed enough concrete evidence on Latham that the district attorney would not hesitate to take action and put the crime lord away for the rest of his life.

It was a simple but ambitious plan, though not one with a swift and easy resolution.

Thankfully, The Wraith was patient. The old man, and others, had taught him well. No matter how long it took to get to Latham, he would wait. Nothing would deter him from this supreme aim. Besides, there was plenty of other crime in Metro City to keep him occupied while he worked through Latham's insidious criminal web. If he kept at it, never gave up, he knew that, eventually, one of them would turn and the process would begin, and Latham's downfall would be the ultimate prize.

* * * * * *

The Wraith took to the rooftops with glee. It was the only time he felt alive.

From above, Metro City shone like a cave filled with diamonds at night. The lights from the buildings twinkled like stars against the hum of the city. Streaks of light crisscrossed the urban sprawl, headlights and brake lights giving the illusion of life to the city Paul loved.

It wasn't until he got closer to the ground that the ugliness of Metro City reared its head.

A woman's shrill cry cut through the night and The Wraith was on the move.

Like lightning, he leapt from rooftop to rooftop until he stood on a building ledge and peered over. In the dimly lit alley below, two men mugged a young couple. The male victim was face down in the filth, either unconscious or dead; it was hard to tell from above. The woman put up a fight but, outnumbered two to one, she fought a losing battle. Her attackers taunted her, toying with her like a cat would a mouse before pouncing.

The Wraith attached a hook and line to the ledge, verified it was secure, then leapt off the roof into empty space.

"Step away from her!" he shouted as the descender controlled and slowed his fall. His cape expanded and he brought the Eyes of Judgment to life.

No longer interested in the woman, the thugs turned their attention toward the newcomer. One of them pulled a pistol and aimed it at the thing dropping from the sky. The Wraith wrapped his cape around himself. The man pulled the trigger three times.

Nothing happened.

The Wraith alighted on the cracked concrete as though he had flown down from above. The descender rig ejected as he walked toward the two men and their prey, his cape still tightly wrapped around him.

The man with the gun fired twice more.

Again, nothing.

He continued to pull the trigger and quickly expended his bullets.

The gunman shouted something anatomically impossible at The Wraith while his friend, who was obviously the brains of their partnership, ran.

The Wraith threw out a hand and three tiny, almost imperceptible projectiles launched toward the running man. They hit him in the back, shoulder and leg, and he dropped hard to the pavement, convulsing as fifty thousand volts coursed through his body.

The gunman remained belligerent.

"Drop the gun," The Wraith said.

The gunman stood firm, clearly not wishing to back down, but not really knowing what to do next. So, he did nothing but stand there, flashing an angry face at the Dread Avenger. Then, having made a decision, he rushed at The Wraith, preferring fight over flight. The Wraith reacted with a spinning scissor kick to the head, ending the fight before it began.

"Are you okay, Miss?" The Wraith asked gently as the woman knelt beside her fallen partner.

She nodded, too frightened to speak.

The Wraith crouched next to the injured man, removed a glove and felt for a pulse. He let out a sigh of relief when he found one. He tapped his cowl at his right temple, activating the in-cowl radio that put him into contact with his team back in the Lair.

"I need you to have an ambulance sent to my location," The Wraith said. "We have a man with severe head trauma and a woman suffering from mild shock. I'm also leaving a couple of...gentlemen...gift-wrapped for Metro PD. Can you alert them to this fact?"

He turned to the woman. She seemed as afraid of him as the men who attacked her.

"It's okay. Help is on the way," he assured her.

"Tha...thank you," she said.

He merely smiled in reply.

The Wraith tied up both men and promptly left, not wishing to be around when the emergency services personnel arrived.

He pointed his grapnel gun aloft and, with the click of a button, headed skyward toward the rooftops as though he could fly.

The young lady had been the first non-criminal to get a good long view of The Wraith. With her testimony, the press began talking about the vigilante Dread Avenger roaming the streets of Metro City more than anything else. Ironically, it was this news item, and this alone, that finally took Paul Sanderson off the front and gossip pages. He was no longer headline news at all, and The Wraith's legend grew and proved anything but forgotten.

* * * * * *

The fight continued.

For a further two years, The Wraith fought to stem the tide of crime, and simultaneously hurt Robert Latham as much as possible.

He was only partially successful.

Metro City was a hothouse of evil and corruption. Once, so very long ago, it had been a beacon to the world, an example of what a city this size could be, but like so many others before, the disease of crime and corruption took root. Like weeds in a neglected lawn, eventually the crime lords and crooked officials took over. Metro City became a cesspool of graft and greed. Building projects were halted, never to be completed. Families were kicked out of their homes, the city's waterways were polluted, and it wasn't safe to walk down the street at night, alone or in a group.

That was before The Wraith hit the scene.

Crime in Metro City had decreased dramatically since The Wraith's crusade began. Corruption within local government had also started to change thanks to Metro City's savior uncovering secret handshake deals, bribery, forgery, extortion, and murder. Thanks to some creative bookkeeping and the creation of a shell company or twelve, there was also an influx of capital being funneled into the campaign coffers of honest politicians and organizations whose sole purpose was to help those in need. But it was slow going and, despite it all, corruption still reigned supreme.

None of this good work could be traced back to Paul Sanderson, which was exactly as he planned it. The reclusive millionaire had at first faded to the back pages of the newspapers, then was no longer mentioned at all. The odd invitation to attend an event or two in Metro City still arrived at the door from time to time, but they had become a trickle and, Paul knew, would eventually stop altogether.

At home, Paul's life remained as it had been when he started his war on crime. He spent most of his waking hours either working in the Lair, or reading in the low light of his library. After some further months, he finally allowed Simpson to transfer his clothing to the home's main bedroom suite. Sanderson House was his now and it was time to stop living under the shadow of his parents' memories.

Simpson beamed when he was told this, no doubt considering the move a small victory.

Every so often, there would again be a small mention or article about the reclusive Paul Sanderson in the papers or a magazine. *What Had Become of Paul Sanderson? Where and Who is Paul Sanderson?* were but some of the headlines. It was hard for the media to imagine a person who would not only shun the spotlight but also prefer to remain sequestered away from the world at large.

As far as Paul was concerned, as long as crime and corruption remained, Paul Sanderson would remain in seclusion so The Wraith could do his good work. In fact, when he once thought long and hard about it, he realized that, for all intents and purposes, Paul Sanderson had perished in Africa. Without his parents, without Judy Hess or the old man, there was really nothing left for Paul Sanderson to live for. But The Wraith? He had his mission to live for. Nothing else mattered.

He had a city to save.

~ Chapter 17 ~

It started out as a night like any other. Once the sun went down, The Wraith's work began.

The city was surprisingly quiet this night, which always made him nervous. His efforts were indeed having an impact, but after a couple of years, Robert Latham was still not behind bars and corruption was still rife within the Metro PD.

Ultimately, it frustrated him.

For all the good he had done, for all the criminals he had taken off the streets, his main goal was not yet achieved. The city was safer, yes, but there was still so much crime, still so much graft and greed. Sometimes the constant effort to stem the tide began to wear him down. In times like this, he even wondered if he made any difference at all. Negative thoughts began to infiltrate his mind more and more. In his more lucid moments, he mulled whether it was simply exhaustion, or whether there was something else going on, something else troubling him. Either way, his frustrations were starting to eat away at him, and even he knew that no good would come of it.

With the city quiet, The Wraith perched on a small building near Hyde Park. He always liked the park. It was the one part of the city where some semblance of peace and quiet could be found. It was the only place he could find within the inner city to even partially replicate the sensations of Africa that he remembered. He briefly wondered if the unease he felt was a yearning to return to that battle-scarred land, perhaps to find some peace with Sam and his family. As quickly as such a thought entered his head, he forced it out just as swiftly. Such a life was not for him. He could not leave the mission unfulfilled. Such an act would destroy him.

Feet dangling over the roof's edge, he enjoyed a snack. Despite his objections, Simpson had started tucking small bags of water and crackers in his belt pouches. To stave off yet another argument about his health, Paul agreed to take snack breaks if it would appease his friend and get him to back off a bit. It worked, not that he would admit it, but Simpson had been right. An occasional break, even when at war, was needed and justified.

Hyde Park was fairly quiet at night these days, which made it perfect for The Wraith. He liked the quiet and often meditated on this rooftop near the park before returning home each morning.

Due to his mounting frustrations and feeling of unease, his thoughts had started turning toward the future. He was beginning to wonder just how much of a future he actually had. Being The Wraith took a toll on him both physically and mentally. He would never admit this to either Simpson or Max, but on his own, deep down, he knew a breakdown loomed. Or worse. Far worse.

Paul had started putting plans in motion for the day when he might need to find a suitable replacement, a backup if all went wrong and The Wraith fell in battle. He knew the powers of the Eyes of Judgment, as well as everything else, could be passed on to another worthy recipient. Now all he had to do was find the right person to bear such an incredible weight. So far, he had rejected all of the potential candidates he had considered.

The search continued...until recently. One name came to the fore above the rest.

That night, others had ventured out as well. It was a nice night, warm, but with just enough breeze to add a slight nip to the air. There was also a hint of rain teasing the night sky.

The Wraith watched using a pair of small binoculars procured from his belt a young couple walking through Hyde Park. They were young and obviously very much in love. They held hands as they strolled, talking softly about this or that, sometimes the man whispered something into her ear, or kissed her on her cheek. The woman laughed at something the man said a few times.

They looked happy.

Paul couldn't remember the last time he had been happy. Truly happy. Had he ever been so? It had been even longer since he'd felt the touch of a woman who looked at him the way the woman in the park looked at her man.

He missed that, but knew it was never to be. Such a life was not for him. He had long ago accepted that.

The Wraith dropped down into the street and crept into the park, never losing sight of the couple he had been watching so closely. As he followed them, he stuck to the shadows, remaining hidden from view. The man was really the one he was studying, the latest candidate to perhaps serve as his replacement if needed.

His name was Michael Reeve. He was a police officer, one of the few trustworthy cops to wear a MPD badge. On the surface, he appeared to be exactly as advertised—an honest cop, a devoted boyfriend and an all-around nice guy. He was an orphan, without any kith or kin save his girlfriend. Her name was Leena Patterson and they were clearly happy together.

* * * * * *

The full moon had risen about an hour before a classic Daimler sedan came to a halt in an alley in the dingy warehouse district of Metro City. A slight breeze swept through between the buildings, bringing with it pieces of trash and filth.

Inside the car, the driver, Max Horton, lit a match. The light also brought into view the rear passenger—The Wraith. Max lit his cigarette.

"Wait here," The Wraith said, his voice raspy and deep.

"Sure thing, Chief," Max said. "You sure you don't need me to stand point?"

The Wraith silently exited the car. "I shouldn't be long if that tip-off proves to be accurate. Stand by."

And with that, the Dread Avenger exited and moved forward into the darkness.

* * * * * *

Sometime later, Max furrowed his weather-beaten brow and lit another cigarette. Puffing away, he looked about him, trying to remain alert, but the alley appeared deserted. Thinking to check behind the car, he turned his head and saw The Wraith seated in the back seat.

The cigarette dropped from his mouth. He scrambled to get it back between his teeth before he burned himself. "Geez! You nearly gave me a—"

"Drive," The Wraith said firmly.

He saw The Wraith's terrible wounds. "You're wounded. We need to get you—"

"It's too late for that." He wheezed heavily. "Drive. It's time. I can feel it, feel the energy building for release." The Wraith stopped for another breath. "You know where to go. You...you know the plan."

* * * * * *

"Stop here," The Wraith said.

Max did as instructed. He parked the car close to the apartment building where Michael Reeve lived at the mouth of a typical Metro City alley. A pre-arranged plan had been devised in case the unthinkable happened and The Wraith was mortally wounded before the mission was completed. Max had been in on the plan from the beginning, but he'd made it clear to Paul he did not like it. Not one bit.

"Let me help you," Max pleaded, turning to face his friend still seated in the Daimler's back seat.

The Wraith clapped him on the shoulder. "You've helped me more than you will ever know, my friend." He coughed. "What I do next, I must do alone. Your job comes after. You know what to do. What you *must* do."

"I don't want...I...yes...I know what must be done," Max said, his head lowered.

The Wraith weakly smiled and then he was gone. He had an unfortunate date with destiny.

The Wraith staggered into the dark alley and came into the light of the full moon, his black cape no longer cloaking him in darkness, no longer shielding the Eyes of Judgment on his chest. Moving forward, he slumped against the wall to his left, panting and heaving. For what seemed an eternity, he rested there. Then, gathering his strength, he continued forward.

Coming to the end of the alleyway, The Wraith looked up into the night sky. The corpulent moon was almost blinding in its brightness. He reached for the ladder to the fire escape and pulled. With a tired groan, the ladder lowered to the ground. He gasped, discomfort enveloping him as he began his ascent. He slowly worked his way upwards.

At the top, The Wraith tried to climb over the balcony's railing but stumbled and fell onto several potted plants and lay there. He gathered his strength once more. In the weak balcony light, his injuries became clear. Blood oozed from a deep wound to his chest, the blood having splattered onto his arms where he had tried to stop its flow. His right shoulder was wounded just as badly.

Rising—barely—The Wraith eyed the sliding door leading into the apartment. One step forward. Another. And another. One more and he was there. He furiously banged on the door, panting, barely able to stand on his own strength and waited for a response.

"What the...?" came a voice from within. A light turned on in the apartment, but nothing clear was visible through the curtains.

* * * * * *

The curtains ripped open and Michael Reeve stared silently through the door's glass, face to face with the Dread Avenger of the Underworld.

"Oh my lord," he said in shock.

Without further hesitation, Michael unlocked the door and slid it open. The Wraith took one careful step inside and collapsed to the floor.

Michael was stunned beyond belief. Here was his idol, the man whom nobody, at least nobody he knew, believed in save himself. He had been denigrated for his beliefs and honesty by many of those he worked with for believing in what he was told was no more than a ghost story. But now here was The Wraith in his own apartment.

"You're the...the..." was all he could utter.

The Wraith slowly rose to his knees and Michael saw the horrific wound on his chest.

"You're wounded. You need help," Michael said.

"Must pass it on before...before it's too late," The Wraith said.

Michael helped him to his feet.

"I'll help you to the sofa, then I'm calling for an ambulance," he said.

"No. There is little time left," The Wraith said. "You are the one, Michael Reeve."

"You...you know my name?" Michael stammered.

"You're the one..." He slumped against Michael's chest then raised his hands to Michael's temples. A burst of light and then...

Darkness.

~ Chapter 18 ~

"The Wraith was dead. Long live The Wraith." Paul turned and faced Leena once again. "And, as you know, with his dying breath, Paul Sanderson endowed me with all his powers, memories and emotions, intending to erase Michael Reeve's forever. The rest of the story, how I regained my memories, reunited with you, and took on the guise of Paul Sanderson is well known to you."

He took a deep breath. His tale had finally come to an end.

Standing in the Lair, the current Paul Sanderson, the man who had once been Michael Reeve, placed his—Paul's—father's watch back in its resting place. Perhaps one day he would wear it. Perhaps one day he would feel comfortable doing so. But not today.

"That's some story," Leena said at last, leaning back in her chair and stretching. "Thank you for finally telling it to me.

There was a lot there I didn't know. So much pain and heartache. I worry that you're able to cope with all those memories and emotions."

"I've accepted my life as it now is, and the Michael Reeve side of me balances the Paul Sanderson out. While the initial melding had been less than perfect, it has since become the consummate blending of two minds and souls."

"I don't know how you do it, how you live with it all...but I'm glad you do. I'm glad you are who you are. Michael Reeve or Paul Sanderson, you're the man I love, body and soul."

They embraced, kissing passionately. He knew he was blessed to have Leena by his side. And, despite all the pain and hardship, he was blessed to be The Wraith as well.

Everything had worked out for the best.

* * * * * *

Later that night, The Wraith was back on patrol.

Detective Bob Sloan had alerted him a raid was being planned on Toshi Unlimited based on the intel The Wraith had left for the MPD. Sloan and his partner, Rosa Perez, spearheaded the raid.

Sloan and Perez were both top-notch cops and The Wraith knew they were the best bet to bring down the people behind the smuggling ring the right way now that all the evidence had been assembled. The cops had everything under control, but The Wraith nevertheless wanted to see the collar with his own eyes, so he headed toward Toshi Unlimited's headquarters deep in the heart of Metro City's financial district.

It delighted him to see the good guys winning a battle, if not the war, and it was a nice change to see others doing the work for him.

As he watched on, a thought suddenly occurred to him. There was one thing both Paul Sanderson and Michael Reeve had in common despite their inherent differences—their love for Metro City. Each had grown up on different sides of the track, one born into wealth and privilege, the other far from it. One grew up aloof and unloved, the other less so, despite having been brought up by distant relatives. Yet, both were orphans, and both men had looked at Metro City and saw the same thing.

They saw a city in need of rescue.

The Wraith thought back to the story he told Leena earlier. *She's right*, he told himself. *It's some story all right. The story of another man's life and struggles, of hope and loss, and the creation of a great enemy. Yet, it's my story, too.*

Metro City sparkled like a jewel in the night. How could anyone not look upon this place and not fall in love? But Paul hadn't. Neither had Michael. Together, they might just be able to save her. With Leena, Simpson, and Max by his side, The Wraith knew his story would continue onward.

One day he would redeem Metro City. He would prove Paul Sanderson's death was not in vain.

He looked out over the city. His city.

Metro City was a hothouse of evil and corruption.

It was also his home.

The city needed a protector.

It needed The Wraith, the Dread Avenger of the Underworld.

~ Author's Note ~

This story has been in the works a great many years. I first wrote it, as a comic book storyline, around eight or nine years ago. It was intended as a two-part comic book graphic novel which would finally reveal, after all this time, the true never-before-told origin of the very first Wraith/Paul Sanderson. As readers, naturally, know, the character that bears both names in all of the books (and comics) in the series is actually the *second* man to do so. The origin of Michael Reeve, and how he became The Wraith, was detailed in the very first novel in the series. It was originally never my intention to detail the origins of the original hero that made the ultimate sacrifice in the quest for justice. I always thought a little mystery added to the appeal of the series.

Until now.

Over the years, many readers and fans have asked me about the original Sanderson. Where the powers of the Eyes of Judgment came from. Where does Sanderson's body lie? Where and how did he meet Max Horton? And how did he come to make such a powerful enemy in the Cobra? Well, this book answers all of those questions and then some. I certainly hope it quenches readers appetites and provides them with an exciting thrill ride at the same time. It was a joy and a pleasure to write.

As always, there are some people I'd like to thank. First and foremost, on this occasion, is my hugely talented co-writer, Bobby Nash. When I decided to craft this piece as a collaboration (so I could focus my sole energies on another Wraith novel, *Vendetta*, which is coming soon), Bobby was the *only* writer that came to my mind. He is incredibly talented, and has tackled the character before, in a short story soon to be released in an anthology coming from Airship27. He took my comic book script, and plot treatment, and crafted an incredible tale that exceeded all that I expected and hoped for. So thank you, Bobby, you're the best. Thanks also to my editor, AP Fuchs, for helping us craft this piece to the best it can possibly be. Welcome back to the fold, my friend. And a little nod goes to Ed de Santis for the name Abdelkrim.

Special thanks must also go to my Trinity Comics team. You always make me look better than I am. You guys are the best in the biz. And, I'd also like to thank my wife, Jennifer, and our families, particularly through this recently difficult time we've just faced together. I love you all so very much. Good will come from all this, rest assured of that.

And I'd like to thank you, my dear readers. I do what I do for you, and this book is especially for you all. You specifically asked for this tale, and here it is now. This is all for you. I hope you enjoy it.

Before I head off...the next few pages highlight a sneak peek at the next book in the series, the aforementioned *Vendetta*. Look for that in the coming months.

Take care.

Frank Dirscherl
Wollongong NSW, 2017

I've been a fan of Frank Dirscherl's The Wraith for years. I first became aware of the character when a friend of mine was hired to ink an issue of the comic series. Then, I got to know Frank and picked up the novels. Somewhere in there, Frank and I were both part of a pulp anthology book called *Lance Star: Sky Ranger*. Suffice to say, Frank and I have been friends for a number of years.

That's why it was a big thrill when Frank invited me to join him on this novel that told Paul Sanderson's origin story.

And what a story it is.

It's always fun traveling around the world with cool characters and with this story, I put plenty of miles on these tired old tootsies. I appreciate you taking the journey with us.

Thanks again, Frank. You're the best. I hope I did your characters justice.

To you who picked up this novel, I appreciate it. I hope we can get together again for another adventure.

Happy Reading.

Bobby Nash
Bethlehem GA, 2017

~ Sneak peek ~

Turn the page for a preview of the next novel in the series, *Vendetta*, by Frank Dirscherl.

COMING SOON from Trinity Comics

~ Chapter 1 ~

Robert Latham strode into the ornately designed and furnished study in his Metro City home and moved over to the deep mahogany sideboard and poured himself a Cognac from the crystal decanter there. He sniffed, drank, and gazed at his surrounds. Decorated in much the same fashion as his city office, there were busts of the world leaders throughout history that he so admired. For their strength, their cunning. Their ruthlessness. Caesar, Genghis Khan, Stalin, Mao Ze Dong, George W. Bush and Donald Trump were but some of the specimens there. He took another drink, the delicious Remy Martin clarifying his thoughts, and headed to his desk.

Taking a seat in the plush buttoned leather chair, he hadn't a moment to relax before the phone rang.

"Yes?" he said, indignantly. "Oh, Patrich. Good of you to call. What news?"

He took another sip from his drink, savoring the taste while listening.

"You've dealt with Jones, then? Excellent. Oh dear...another deputy with delusions of grandeur. At least Charlie had some sense of patience, and bided his time before trying anything. I spared Charlie for that reason. He may not have been loyal but at least he was halfway competent. But Jones...he never had a chance." Latham leaned back in his chair and smiled. "You're not going to get any similar ideas now are you, Patrich? I wouldn't be very pleased to have to do away with three deputies in a row. My reputation would take a battering." He paused. "Good, smart boy. Good work tonight, also. Efficient and deadly. Traits I admire. You can go home now. We have a busy day tomorrow."

He hung up before any response could be received.

Leaning forward, he chuckled briefly while reaching for the alabaster cigar case on his desk. As he opened the lid and reached inside, the light instantly dimmed to almost nothing, and a screen dropped down from the ceiling at the far end of the room.

"What the...?!"

"Now, now," a familiar voice emanated seemingly from nowhere and everywhere all at once.

"Charlie?" Latham said, with a mixture of bemusement and anger. "How the he–?"

"Temper, temper," Charlie Grieco said, as his face flashed upon the large screen. Latham's former deputy appeared as always; slickly dressed with a smarmy, arrogant air about him. "Is that any way to greet your old comrade?" He laughed while talking.

"What's going on here, Charlie? How did you get this stuff in here?"

Grieco grinned. "Can the great Robert Latham have forgotten that I was his right-hand man for nearly ten years? That I know all his secrets, inside and out?"

"I changed every passcode, altered all my security procedures as I always do after every..." Latham wheezed.

"Purge?" Grieco chimed in. "Is that how you were about to explain your betrayal of me?"

Latham fumed. "Betrayal of you?! You little worm! You tried to usurp control of my organization for yourself. Thought yourself the new big man of Metro City."

"Because you wouldn't let go!" Grieco screamed. "You didn't know when to step aside and let some fresh blood taste their fair share of power. You delayed me from my destiny. And now it's going to cost you."

Latham recovered his composure, leaned back and lit his cigar, blowing smoke before continuing. "Cost me? You must be insane. I don't know where you are or how you managed to pull this off, but you're a dead man, you hear me. A dead man!"

"Funny," Grieco replied, his smile never leaving him, "I was thinking the same thing about you. You asked before how I managed to achieve my little show for you in your study there. Well, I can't take all the credit, you know. I had a little bit of help. I bumped into an old friend of ours, you see. With my knowledge of your practices, and his...well, his skills, we were able to..."

"Get to the point, Charlie," Latham snapped.

"Hmm...well, why don't I let him tell you about it then."

Grieco stepped out of camera range and was quickly replaced by another man, one Latham knew all too well. Crossfire!

He's alive, Latham thought, genuinely frightened for the first time in his life. *How is this possible?*

His tall, muscular frame filled the screen with an imposing menace. His long blond hair was in a ponytail as it was the last time they had met, and there was that annoying little cross-hairs tattoo on the left side of his neck, but he appeared different as well, outfitted in a formfitting black bodysuit, with bullet pouches crisscrossing both shoulders. Emblazoned at the top of his chest was a small duplicate image of the tattoo, in white, with a smeared, blood-red center dot. As the villain leaned in close to the camera, his heavily tanned and lined face became clearer.

"Latham...by your expression I see you remember me."

Latham found it difficult to breathe. Charlie Grieco and Crossfire, teaming up, somehow able to penetrate the security of his home.

"You're no doubt wondering how I come to be alive, how and why I've teamed up with our mutual friend here," he said, gesturing off camera. "The why I'm sure you can work out for yourself. As to the first question...you're going to take that one unanswered to your grave."

Latham gulped, sweat pouring down his brow. He tried to move but was paralyzed with fear, a feeling completely alien to him. "But, but...my family, don't..."

Grieco re-appeared on the screen to stand alongside the much larger Crossfire, the latter of which produced a small apparatus from his belt.

"Goodbye," Crossfire breathed, while Grieco cackled, pressing a button on the apparatus.

A burst of fiery light shot forth, and then...

Darkness.

* * * * * *

The Latham mansion exploded in an inferno that was almost akin to a nuclear detonation. In seconds, the massive house was reduced to mere rubble, and flames spewed skyward as though the Devil's domain was attempting an invasion of Heaven itself. In minutes, with the sirens of the emergency crews sounding in the distance, the conflagration grew, spreading throughout the grounds of the estate. There was no stopping it.

Crossfire's vengeance had been complete. And satisfied.

* * * * * *

Grieco couldn't contain his joy. He shrieked and danced about like a nerd prancing at the prom with the head cheerleader.

"I did it," he shouted. "He's gone. The old man is finally history, and I'm free to take over the organization. Finally to lead."

He turned to face his new found ally. Crossfire stared back at him with a stern expression belying any joy he might have felt at their success.

"Why so glum?" Grieco said, oblivious to anything other than his own ecstasy. "Your enemy is dead. Your mission is complete. Now you can go home to Cobar, or wherever it was you said you came from. Unless, of course, you want a job in *my* organization. I could use a man with your...skills."

Crossfire remained motionless, merely staring at Grieco for some further seconds before finally speaking. "You think my mission is over? That killing Latham is all that I desire?"

"Well, I...I don't know, I..." Grieco stammered, finally starting to think that the situation may not be quite as he imagined. He took a few steps back.

"Latham was just the beginning," Crossfire barked. "And you were simply a means to an end. And now it is your end."

Grieco gulped. Crossfire lifted a gauntletted arm, smirked, and fired.

* * * * * *

Lead coughed from the miniature automatic weapon secreted within the fabric of the arm of his suit. A powerful uzi-style weapon, it connected with the bullets strapped around his bulky frame, meaning it unlikely he would ever run out of bullets in the short term.

The barrage of bullets tore Grieco's body to shreds. When Crossfire finally relented, bloody pieces of flesh were strewn at his feet. He didn't care. As he had said—a means to an end. All his enemies would suffer the same fate. However, Grieco's remains, and Latham's demise, would send a message to the one enemy he was *really* after. The one who deserved every torture, every cruelty, and then finally, death, more than any other.

The Wraith.

About the Type

Garamond is a group of many old-style serif typefaces, originally those designed by Parisian craftsman Claude Garamond and other 16th century French engravers, and now many modern revivals. Though his name was written as 'Garamont' in his lifetime, the typefaces are generally spelled 'Garamond'. **Garamond Normal**, used in this book, is one of those modern revivals.

~ Also Available ~

The Wraith Adventures #1
THE WRAITH
Frank Dirscherl

In a world not far removed from our own, a city lies ravaged.
Crime overruns its streets; its citizens are helpless. Crime lord
Robert Latham, to the world at large a legitimate businessman,
holds the city in his sway. Fear and intimidation rule throughout.
One man stands above the rest, willing to fight for freedom.
That man is The Wraith.
ISBN: 978-0-646-90689-8

AVAILABLE NOW!

www.trinitycomics.com

The Wraith Adventures #2
VALLEY OF EVIL
Frank Dirscherl

After the horror the Cobra unleashed upon Metro City, Paul
Sanderson has recuperated, regained his strength and focus, and
the city has been rebuilt while its citizens have slowly started to
regroup and move forward. Into this relative calm marches Ma Tzi,
the Hong Kong drug lord, who senses a weakness in resident crime
lord Robert Latham's hold on the city and intends to exploit that
in any way necessary. And at any cost.
ISBN: 978-0-646-90809-0

AVAILABLE NOW!
www.trinitycomics.com

The Wraith Adventures #2.5

CROSSFIRE

Stephen J. Semones; edited by Frank Dirscherl

After a terrorist attack leaves the citizens of Metro City reeling, an enigmatic stranger emerges from the wake of the destruction to wage war on local crime-lord Robert Latham. In the midst of this, Max Horton, The Wraith's right-hand man, vanishes without a trace. Searching for Max, and for those responsible for the devastation, The Wraith sets out for answers.
ISBN: 978-0-646-58377-8

AVAILABLE NOW!

www.trinitycomics.com

The Wraith Adventures #3
CULT OF THE DAMNED
Frank Dirscherl

With the city back firmly in his grasp, crime lord and entrepreneur
Robert Latham is celebrating by bankrolling Metro City's 200th
anniversary gala year, which includes the unveiling of a never-
before-seen ancient Aztec stone carving—the Cortes Stone—at the
City Gallery, a carving that has thrilled the scientific and artistic
communities, but infuriated the monstrous Aztekoth.
ISBN: 978-0-646-90824-3

AVAILABLE NOW!

www.trinitycomics.com

The Wraith Adventures #4
CRY OF THE WEREWOLF
Frank Dirscherl

Having gone through ordeal after ordeal, Paul Sanderson (aka The Wraith Dread Avenger of the Underworld ®) and his love Leena Patterson, decide to take a long overdue vacation. However, their idyll is soon shattered by an attack by a creature nobody thought could possibly exist—a werewolf. Soon, an evil so heinous makes himself known, and only The Wraith could possibly defeat it.
ISBN: 978-0-646-57757-9

AVAILABLE NOW!

www.trinitycomics.com

The Wraith comic book series

THE WRAITH: THE COLLECTED EDITIONS #1-3

Frank Dirscherl and a variety of artists

The adventures of the Dread Avenger of the Underworld in comic book format. The trade paperback collecting issues #1-3 of the series. Including each issue's color cover. Over 100 pages of action and excitement.
ISBN: 978-1-4710-4977-4

AVAILABLE NOW!

www.trinitycomics.com

The Wraith short film on DVD
THE WRAITH: EYES OF JUDGMENT

This Special Edition 2-disc DVD, based on the novel *The Wraith*,
features over four hours of special features spanning two
impressive discs. With animated menus mixed in digital surround
sound, this will satisfy even the most hardcore DVD enthusiasts.
ASIN: B000F3ZTFS

AVAILABLE NOW!

www.trinitycomics.com

Join FRANK DIRSCHERL and Trinity Comics on social media!

facebook.com/publisherTrinityComics

@Trinity_Comics

instagram.com/trinity.comics

trinitycomics.proboards.com

All Trinity Comics, The Wraith and Starflame novels, comics and merchandise can be obtained directly from the Trinity Comics website –
www.trinitycomics.com

Want to be The Wraith?

Well, it might be hard to actually *be* The Wraith, unless of course you, too, have been endowed with the power of the Eyes of Judgment. But you can certainly dress, drink and drive like him [*] (and you don't always have to be a millionaire to do so). See for yourselves.

The Wraith/Paul Sanderson wears:

- tailored clothing from Cad & the Dandy Tailors and Shirtmakers – www.cadandthedandy.co.uk
- bespoke footwear from Gaziano & Girling – www.gazianogirling.com
- watches from Tudor (Tudor Heritage Black Bay 36 and Tudor Heritage Black Bay Blue) www.tudorwatch.com
- Armani Code cologne from Giorgio Armani – www.giorgioarmanibeauty-usa.com/for-him-armani-code/for-him-armani-code,default,sc.html

drinks:

- Twinings Earl & Lady Grey tea – www.twinings.co.uk
- Vittoria coffee – www.vittoria.com
- The Balvenie Scotch whisky – www.thebalvenie.com
- Armand de Brignac champagne – www.armanddebrignac.com
- Cosmopolitan cocktails

---

[*] Please note: Trinity Comics does not condone drinking and driving. **All** adults, please always drink responsibly and never drink and drive

uses:

- Dell laptops - www.dell.com.au
- Chesterfield furniture from Abbey Furniture www.chesterfieldfurnituremelbourne.com.au
- wallets from Launer - www.launer.com
- a Samsung Galaxy A3 cell phone - www.samsung.com/au/consumer/mobile-phone/smartphones/galaxy-a/SM-A300YZKAXSA

drives:

- a Rolls Royce Wraith - www.rolls-roycemotorcars.com/en-GB/wraith.html

And, if you're really eager to actually look like The Wraith—in full costume—then you can always head over to Xtreme Design FX and let Lance Coulter there make you an exact replica of the costume used for The Wraith motion picture - www.xtremedesignfx.com

www.ingramcontent.com/pod-product-compliance
Lightning Source LLC
Chambersburg PA
CBHW032044240626
47154CB00003B/1068